SAVED BY A KNIFE

Uncreated Love Series

Other books by Philip Vianney:
Uncreated Love
Top Secret

The Uncreated Love Series was written to reinforce
Catholic truths through literary fiction.

For more information regarding the Uncreated Love Series
go to uncreatedlove.com

SAVED BY A KNIFE

A Mystery

Uncreated Love Series

Chapter 1

"Is it over yet?" Jennifer asked in a slurred voice, casting blood-shot eyes at the friend sitting with her on a hill. Their knees were bent, one resting her head of brunette curls on crossed forearms and the other twirling the blue-dyed tip of her ponytail. They plucked dry bristle grass to shred with nervous fingers. Bare silver maples, pin oaks, and dogwoods swayed in a cool breeze, having dropped their final rust-colored leaves of the year. A distant tractor pulling a load of hay made it difficult to hear the muffled voices in the valley.

Allison glanced over her shoulder at the cemetery below, where a few dozen mourners stared at a shiny casket above a dark hole. While some dabbed their eyes with tissues, others wrapped arms around each other. Between the cries of a red-tailed hawk, she answered: "They're listening to the minister reading from a thick book." *Fall is such an appropriate backdrop for a funeral,* she thought, noticing signs of life in nature withering away. Her voice cracked, "I still can't believe this happened to Dana … in our little town!"

Jennifer wiped a stream of tears and eye makeup away. "I'll miss her. Even though it ended on a bad note, we sure had a lot of good times at the mall and parties this year."

"Shouldn't we join the crowd?" Allison prompted despite mixed feelings about the idea. She was living with her fourth foster family and had no experience handling herself at a funeral. "Looks like everyone from our junior class is down there, even our teachers and principal."

"Probably."

But neither girl moved—too numb, too unsure how to slip in, too worried how they'd be received.

Jennifer knew it was her place to be at the Berryville funeral home earlier this morning and now this graveside service, but the traumatic circumstances of her friend's death made it too difficult. The bloody image of Dana lying on her bedroom floor three days ago made it impossible to go through the expected protocols. It just wasn't the same as when her father's parents died of lung and pancreatic cancer years ago. "Pass the 'lemonade,'" she said, referring to the vodka she'd taken from her mom's liquor cabinet and mixed with an 8-ounce bottle of lemonade.

"I think you've had enough."

"I'm not driving."

"I'd say not, but I don't want to carry you home."

But Jennifer impulsively reached across her friend for the thermos.

After a moment's struggle, Allison relented. "OK, but only if you tell me what it felt like holding the dead body."

Jennifer took a gulp and coughed a little. "It wasn't a *body* I held, but *Dana*. She felt cold and limp … not ice cold but definitely not warm. She felt heavy, too. It was a really weird feeling holding a dead person, like a bad dream. I wondered if it was really her because she looked so pale. You know, we walk around most of the time like we control the world and will live forever, but we deceive ourselves."

Allison said "Hmm" in response and looked back again. "It looks like they're praying—their heads are bowed."

Jennifer asked in a serious tone, "Do you think their prayers are being heard?"

Allison started giggling. "God only knows!"

Jennifer's purse sailed through the air in the vicinity of Allison. Although Jennifer aimed for Allison's face, her motor skills were so impaired that she missed horribly. Striving to keep a straight face, she remarked, "How can you joke at a time like this?"

Allison was unmoved by Jennifer's pathetic display of civility. "How can I not joke at a time like this?"

The pair laughed nervously, which soothed the pain for another minute or two.

Allison heard footsteps and warned: "Don't look now, but Mr. Keller is headed our way. Jennifer, you're in no condition to talk. Just cry and nod your head. If you do that, everything will be fine."

Jennifer said sarcastically, "Look at the bright side. He's missing his right arm, which means he can only drag one of us away."

"You're horrible," Allison responded.

It took several minutes for Dana's father, Tim, to reach them, and his face was rosy. The girls scooted around to face him. He was a large, burly man, so the climb was a challenge. The storms of life had made him a gruff man, not likable by many residents of Berryville, and Jennifer and Allison were among them.

When Tim caught his breath, the first thing he noticed was bloodshot eyes. "Girls, how are you?" he asked out of habit, although he was only there to deliver a message.

Mumbling "OK," Jennifer covered her face to convey no interest in holding a conversation.

After an awkward pause, Tim continued, "Jennifer, Detective Peterson has been trying to find you since the police came to my house. He told me yesterday that he called your mom to make sure you go to the police station in the morning and that if I saw you at the funeral, to let you know."

Jennifer only lifted her head enough to say, "She texted me. I'll be there tomorrow."

"All right, then," Tim said, satisfied.

Allison waited until he walked away to get into his truck, then quipped with a laugh, "It official! You're a functional alcoholic! You did great!"

As Jennifer ignored the sarcasm, Allison became alarmed. "Bad news! The new guy in school, John, is coming to visit us. Put your seat belt on for a sermon."

However, Jennifer sat up straight and tried in vain to look more sober. "He's an old friend who just transferred to Berryville High," she said defensively.

"How can he be an old friend? Didn't he just move here a couple of months ago?"

"John went to a Catholic boys' boarding school a couple years ago," Jennifer said. "Actually, we were really close before he left. He wasn't on Facebook or Twitter, but we e-mailed and texted a lot."

Allison gave her an inquisitive look. "Strange. I've never seen him hang out with you in the past couple of months—he only hangs out with the church crowd."

"Back in junior high we went in different directions but made an effort to stay friends."

Sizing up the scene as he approached, John decided to keep his visit short. "Hey," he greeted them and then turned back toward the casket being lowered and covered with black dirt. "Jen, if you want to talk, you know where to find me."

"Thanks, John," said Jennifer while Allison burped. Jennifer kicked Allison discreetly and gave her a fierce look for her rudeness.

Without saying another word, John started back down the hill.

Allison took a final assessment of the scene and said dramatically: "Look at Peter. It appears he's shedding a tear for the TV reporter's camera."

Jennifer didn't look but fumed interiorly at the mention of her ex. *He's so vain!*

Now maintenance workers were filling in the gravesite. Allison asked the most pressing question on their minds, "Who do you think killed her?"

"I have no idea," Jennifer answered honestly.

Chapter 2

When Jennifer arrived at Scott Peterson's office, he was completing paperwork, a task that annoyed him more with each passing year. He frequently complained to his circle of family and friends that policemen needed to be out "catching bad guys, not pushing papers behind a desk."

Before him sat a distraught seventeen-year-old who posed no mystery to him. Twenty-four years on the police force had exposed him to criminals of all ages, shapes, and sizes. He applied the maxim "justice is supposed to be blind" to his detective work. Although this glamorous teenager didn't seem to fit the profile of a brutal murderess, all that mattered to him were facts.

Detective Peterson greeted Jennifer callously, "Miss Lawson, thank you for taking the time to come to the police station. I hope I'm not inconveniencing you."

No "Sorry that your friend is dead"? Jennifer was stunned. She sat quietly, looking down at her shoes after brief eye contact with the detective. Her silent reply could be attributed to the fact that she had already given her account of the murder to the police and found the same questions annoying. In addition, her hangover was affecting her state of mind.

"Can you think of anyone who might have murdered Dana?" Detective Peterson asked.

"No."

"Did you and Dana have a disagreement earlier that day at school in which you told her that you 'hated her'?"

"Yes," replied Jennifer, embarrassed about her short temper

and immature last words to Dana. *Who told him that? Only a few classmates were present when we had that fight.*

"Is it true that your long-time boyfriend, Peter Wilson, broke up with you a couple of days before the murder and started dating Dana?" As the detective pressed on, Jennifer fumed inside, *"It's none of your damn business!"* but instead reacted without any emotion, "Yes." Part of her wanted to say that their relationship was at the end of the rope anyway. Her feelings toward Peter had weakened, and the only reasons she hung around him were because a new boyfriend hadn't shown up yet and she enjoyed being with his powerful family, playing tennis with the governor and getting expensive gifts from his mom, who shopped high-end fashion stores. But these reasons sounded too complicated and shallow, so she decided not to elaborate.

Jennifer wondered if Peter had shared this information about his new girlfriend with the detective since it wasn't public knowledge yet. Also, Peter was in the crowd that overheard Jennifer telling Dana that she hated her. Since Peter cruelly and unexpectedly broke up with Jennifer days before the murder, she assumed he was the informant. *Peter, you jerk!*

"Miss Lawson, your fingerprints are the only ones we found on the knife." Detective Peterson paused to read the girl's body language.

Jennifer didn't flinch as she said confidently, "I already told you that I pulled the knife out of her when I found her in her bedroom. I should have just called 911, but I must have thought I could help save her."

The detective leaned forward. "Officer Carlos Manuel said he heard you say 'Why did I do it?' at the scene of the crime."

"I told you the crime scene was a blur to me. I was in shock while I held Dana's corpse. I don't remember saying anything of the sort. I had nothing to do with the murder."

The detective ignored her defense, concluding: "You're the only one with a motive. We have a confession. We have the murder weapon. Since you're only seventeen, any further questioning will be postponed at this time. I'm going to ask your parents to get you an attorney if they haven't already. The DA will soon receive my recommendation that you be indicted for the murder of Dana Keller. That's all for now."

Chapter 3

The following day, the temperature was too low and the sky too gloomy to make Benton Park inviting. Except for a couple of diehard joggers, it would have been empty. Jennifer sat alone on the park bench overlooking the lake, smelling chimney smoke while she waited for John to get off work at the local music store, where he taught guitar lessons. Over the years, the park was their favorite meeting place.

John wasn't one of her party friends but rather a confidant. Like everyone in life, Jennifer needed someone to talk to about personal and private things. She had no siblings or close cousins, and her relationship with her workaholic parents was estranged. Without family support and fleeting friends who could not be trusted, John was a treasure to her. He could keep a secret and was a stable element in her life over the years. They simply enjoyed a plutonic relationship.

In particular, Jennifer was enchanted with how John understood the deeper things in life. Attendance for two years at a minor seminary enabled him to see things in a way she could not. His grasp of philosophy was a fresh change compared with the superficial talk at school, music, and TV shows she was bombarded with all day long.

What happened several years ago that hindered their friendship? There is a decision in life that everyone has to make, consciously or not. This decision is what separated John and Jennifer and made them feel as if they were worlds apart.

As she waited for John, she wondered why he was always quiet at school. Was he more reserved than quiet? She couldn't tell. It didn't matter; all she knew was that John had proven to be trustworthy over the years, and his advice in personal matters was always helpful.

John took a seat on the far end of the bench. "Hi there!"

Jennifer smiled warmly. "Hey, thanks for meeting me last night. I know that I laid a lot of heavy things on you, but I appreciate that you were there for me. When the detective accused me of murder, I almost fell apart."

John corrected her, teasing, "Almost fell apart? No, you did fall apart."

Jennifer stared at him while his gaze focused on a distant point on the horizon. "Anyway, thank you. It means a lot to me that you believe I didn't do it. You're the only person in the world who believes in my innocence."

"You're welcome."

"Why are you always there for me?"

John raised his eyebrows and said dramatically, "It's a great act of charity on my part to help you navigate through the treacherous waters of life."

"How big of you!" Jennifer retorted sarcastically.

John was silent, so she turned her attention to the crinkly burning bush and fading mums nearby. She reminisced about the spectacular fall colors that glowed just a couple of weeks earlier. "I wish the fall colors lasted longer!"

"You wouldn't appreciate the beauty as much if it lasted longer but instead would get bored with it. Haven't you noticed that most of the good things in life only fill our time for brief moments, and then the rubrics of everyday life fill the rest? I think God does this to wet our whistle for something greater than this life." John finally turned his head and smiled at Jennifer. "It's a good sign that you like true beauty."

He's setting me up. Jennifer returned a cautious smile. "Why?"

"Beauty is one of the three things God is made up of," John said.

I hope I don't regret asking this. "What are the other two?"

"Truth and love."

What is truth? And if love is supposed to last forever, then I've never known love. "Don't get your hopes up too high for me because I only appreciate beauty, and I suspect that it's not enough to get me to heaven," Jennifer said.

John was surprised that she made a comment about the afterlife. "That's the first time in my life I heard you mention the word heaven."

I told you not to get your hopes up for me. "You know what I think heaven will be like? It will be like the simple days when we were twelve. Remember when our two families took that camping vacation? I don't think I've felt so much joy in my life." *Maybe because a couple of months later Mom and Dad separated, which destroyed our family.*

John protested her account of the camping vacation: "We woke up to soggy French toast! The first day we had to drag our canoes down the river because of the drought! Dinner was hot dogs that had fallen into the ashes, and we forgot to bring toothpaste so the ashes just sat between our teeth for days."

Jennifer teased back, "But the lightning show that one night was beautiful!"

John shook his head in a dramatic gesture of disbelief. "Yes, the lightning was spectacular for about 20 minutes until the squall line hit. I remember the girls heading for the cars while the guys labored in a torrential downpour, ankle deep in mud, trying to save all the camping stuff. That campout was a nightmare!" John joked, "If that vacation is what heaven will be like, please pass me some of that special lemonade you like so much."

John's joke about her spiked lemonade caught her completely by surprise. Instead of getting defensive, Jennifer enjoyed an innocent, heart-filled laugh. *It feels so good to be in his company. I'll miss him.* "But you have to admit the lightning show was beautiful!" she continued.

John's eyes returned to the horizon as he reflected on her words, seeing that reminiscing was her coping mechanism. *What tremendous pain she must be feeling right now.* "You're right, the lightning storm was beautiful. Thanks for reminding me to stay focused on the beautiful things in life."

Jennifer stared at him. *I wish he'd look at me right now.* "I asked you to meet me today so that I could thank you for being my friend over the years. Please forget all my shortcomings and focus on the good times we've shared." Jennifer leaned over and kissed his check before departing.

Chapter 4

The Charlie Biton gubernatorial campaign had a makeshift calling center for its headquarters, stuffed with dozens of eager volunteers. With the election just fourteen days away, there was little time left to sway voters' minds and even less for sleep. Thousands of details and endless phone calls had the staff working frantically.

Eleanor Smith, a veteran campaign manager, prided herself on always running a well-orchestrated campaign. This wasn't a job to her but a mission in life. In fact, her friends nicknamed her "the missionary." Her calling wasn't feeding the poor, building affordable housing, or collecting donations of clothing but instead doing something she considered more noble—securing reproductive rights for all.

Jim Hilton, Eleanor's aide, walked anxiously toward Eleanor's office. His agitated countenance was unnoticed because of all the commotion surrounding him. He looked at Belinda, Eleanor's personal intern. "Is The Witch in?" he asked cautiously.

Belinda shot him a disapproving look but knew the name fit all too well. "She's busy."

"I have something very important," Jim said, waving an envelope impatiently. "What's she doing?"

"Talking to a friend."

Jim barged into Eleanor's office and found her talking on the phone with her feet up, high heels off.

Eleanor waved to him that she needed a minute to end her phone call, but Jim rushed over to her and snatched the phone from her hand. He barked, "She'll call you back soon" and took pleasure in hanging up.

"That was rude. Let me remind you—you're only my aide. This had better be important or your head will roll."

And everyone knows you've rolled a lot of heads. Jim stood there unmoved by her threats. He knew too many secrets, and she knew it. Both of them realized that if he were terminated, she would have to use a body bag for the job. Although the thought crossed her mind from time to time, this was not one of them. "I was opening the stack of unread mail addressed to you and came across a letter from your young friend Dana Keller. You'd better read this for yourself."

Jim handed over the letter as he recalled the conversations he had with Dana. She was a teenager who dropped in on Eleanor occasionally. Their conversations were always private. Although Jim suspected something illegal was going on, he had no proof.

Eleanor looked at the letter. It was the same letter Dana sent to Eleanor's home address ten days earlier. *She sent it to both of my addresses!* She pretended to slowly read it as if she was unaware of its contents. Eleanor had hoped to go to her grave alone with this secret, but now Jim might have to go to his grave sooner than expected.

Four months earlier, Eleanor was sent to Berryville to dig up dirt on Governor Jack Wilson. She was desperate to secure a win for the Biton campaign, regardless of the cost. She was spying on Peter Wilson, the governor's son, and his girlfriend Jennifer when she met Dana and became aware of her interest in heroin.

At first, Eleanor was satisfied with innocent feedback on the governor's family in return for drugs. At the beginning, Eleanor provided an abundance of powdered white heroin without asking for much in return. This new influx on money and drugs quickly spiraled Dana into a hardcore addict. Over time, Eleanor demanded more and more information. Because addicts are known to betray friends and family to fuel their addictions, Eleanor's goal in having a spy was achieved.

Eleanor decided to consider this problem from a different angle. It occurred to her that Jim knowing this secret might be a blessing. Now she could send him on an errand that she couldn't do with the election so close. She could decide what to do with Jim once the mission was over.

Her eyes drifted slowly to the bottom of the letter to give the impression she was finishing it. She set the letter down while she pondered her next step. A fake display of shock filled her face as she considered her next move. "It seems like our Berryville spy double-crossed us."

Jim displayed slight anger. "She'll have a price to pay for betraying you."

Eleanor put on a devilish smile. "Not in this world."

"What do you mean?" Jim asked unaware of the small town's latest news.

"She was murdered seven days ago," Eleanor said matter-of-factly.

"Who would do such a thing to that beautiful, young lady?" His eyes fixed on Eleanor to try to read her thoughts. *Did she kill Dana? Human life is cheap to her, so I wouldn't put it past her.*

Uncomfortable with what might be going through Jim's mind, Eleanor looked at Dana's letter again. "Heaven only knows," she quipped to avoid a direct answer. After a pause, she continued, "Dana had two things of interest to us, the information on Peter Wilson, which would secure a win for us, and secretly recorded conversations that could hurt Biton. We need to retrieve her iPhone and laptop. With the election only 2 weeks away, we have to move fast."

From the letter it appears that this information would damage you the most. Jim didn't like the sound of this conversation. "What do you propose?" he asked, stressing the word "propose" because he knew Eleanor hated it when a man used that word with her. Multiple failed marriages over the years had caused misandry, hatred of men, in her. Eleanor's deceptive personality fooled most people, but not Jim.

"Maybe you could poke around and see what you can find. You need to work fast because the election is 2 weeks away."

"What do you suggest I do?" Jim asked, thinking *I wish I was recording this conversation.*

"Get Dana's laptop and phone. I would suggest you monitor Jennifer Lawson for information. If you get caught, we never had this conversation."

"Of course."

"Grab all the bugging equipment from the safe. Remember the stuff we used to bug the governor's vacation home last summer. Arrange an expensive arrangement of flowers to be sent to Jennifer's home with a note signed 'Sorry for your loss, Dad.' Insist with the florist you want to see the flower piece before it's delivered. When reviewing it, slip the transmitting device under the moss.

"What's in it for me?"

The chance to live another day if you're lucky and if I'm having a good day. But Eleanor stated: "If you're successful, Charlie will win the election. Since he's down in the polls, he'll view you as the hero who saved the day. I'll see to it that you become the governor's personal aide."

Liar. If I get this info from Dana, I'll go to Charlie myself. Jim faked a gracious reply, "Thanks for your confidence in me. I won't let you down." He picked up Dana's letter and envelope. "I'll keep you posted on my progress."

Chapter 5

Several hours after being in the park with John, Jennifer was in her room. She signed the letter she just finished composing and placed it on the dresser, next to the weekly envelope of cash that her mother had given her for shopping and other recreational spending. Her iPod was playing soft rock music that reminded her of better days. It was music from the 1970's and 1980's her parents listened to before their divorce ... Fleetwood Mac, REO Speedwagon, Bruce Springsteen, and so on.

One last look in the mirror confirmed that the elegant, full-length nightgown was the right choice. She turned and walked over to her handbag on the bed. The bottle of sleeping pills was waiting.

Everything is ready. Mom, I wish I could talk to you; wish I felt close to you.

A faint tapping sound was heard from the window. Without looking at the window, Jennifer replied, "Not tonight, Allison!"

John smiled and tapped again.

Jennifer looked in disbelief and saw that John, of all people, was tapping at her window. A slight sense of shame filled her heart knowing that John almost witnessed her suicide attempt. She had to force a smile as she opened her bedroom window. "Most people use the front door."

"I tried but no one answered." John sensed an unspoken anxiety disturbing her. He thought a little humor might lighten the mood. He decided to comment on the ladder, which he found placed at the foot of her window sill, concealed by a hedge of evergreen bushes outlining the back of her house.

"The fire marshal would be proud of you for keeping an escape ladder at your bedroom window."

Despite the severity of the situation and her mood, a small grin formed on Jennifer's lips. She was about to correct him that the ladder was placed there to aid her returning to her bedroom but decided silence would be a better reply. It was comforting to know that John always presumed the best regarding her behavior, although she sensed he saw right through her. "You can come in at your own risk."

John hadn't planned on a bedroom rendezvous. The thought of entering her bedroom while she was dressed in a nightgown was not an option he wanted to entertain. "Thanks, but I'm fine here. I'll only be a minute."

He is so weird at times. Jennifer raised her eyebrows in playful suspense. "Then what do you want?"

"After our meeting at the park, I went to church to pray for you. Something didn't seem right, and I was worried about you. After a couple of hours of prayer, I heard a voice speak to my heart. It was a message for you. I didn't hear an audible word but more like a conviction in my heart."

With a touch of mockery, Jennifer replied cynically, "Don't tell me. The message is that 'God loves me.' "

He tried to keep a straight face as he replied, "If I was a betting man—though I'm not—I would probably bet that God loves you, but that's not what the message was."

Jennifer smirked at his joke. "Can't this wait till tomorrow?"

"Interesting that you ask that question because that's the exact question I asked, and I felt a sense of urgency come over me."

"If you think you hear voices, then you need to see a doctor with a couch," Jennifer said sarcastically.

John's eyes were drawn to her neatly made bed. Her headboard had about a half dozen pillows piled high. On one edge of the bed sat her handbag, which captured his attention. "Do you ever sense something wrong?"

"What do you mean?" Jennifer was intrigued.

"When I look at you, I see something good, but when I look at your handbag, I sense something wrong. May I look in it?" John asked.

"No!" *Did he say that he sees something good in me?*

His eyes noticed an unmarked envelope on her dresser. "Let me tell you what the voice told me in prayer, and then I'll be on my way."

"OK." Jennifer's heart raced.

"God wanted me to tell you to have hope; don't despair." Looking back at the handbag, he asked, "Is there something in there to help you commit suicide?"

Jennifer stared at him disbelievingly, hugging herself with her arms, and shivered. *How does he know about the bottle of sleeping pills in my handbag? I didn't tell anyone. Did that voice tell him?*

She glanced at the untouched suicide note safely tucked in the envelope. Although it was within grasp of John, she concluded that he hadn't discovered her secret from her suicide note.

Her curiosity was getting the best of her, so she asked "Why don't you come in so we can talk? It's beginning to freeze in here."

"Why don't you put a robe on if you're cold?"

In a tone of playful frustration, she replied. "I'll be right back." Jennifer knew there was only one condition John had in their friendship—that she not dress "hot" in his presence. She knew she had to leave the mini-skirts and crop tops hanging in her closet when they hung out together. At first this detail annoyed her, but in time she was happy to make this little sacrifice for him.

She never knew exactly why he demanded this of her. Did he find her irresistible when she wore a mini-skirt? Maybe he didn't want to be attracted to her? The question of why she needed more than a nightgown to be in his presence tonight baffled her as she grabbed a full-length robe from the closet. When she turned around she noticed John holding the envelope with her suicide note still tucked in it.

"May I read this?"

Jennifer closed her eyes and consented with a slight nod.

Jennifer saw a strength in John she didn't see in other young men. Although both he and Peter had a masculine build, John had a moral strength that Peter lacked. An interior stability and peace about him made him strong in other ways; whereas, Peter was a directionless playboy. It wasn't that John was predictable, but whatever he did had good motives. Whoever trusted John had no fear of being hurt. Jennifer never saw this quality in any other men she knew, not even her father. Such rare integrity made her feel safe in his presence.

When John finished reading her suicide note, he broke the silence. "It was a good gesture on your part to attempt to remove any guilt your parents would have felt. Why don't you let me try to help you?"

Jennifer replied to his question by offering him a blank stare.

One would suspect Jennifer's pending suicide was due to being falsely accused of Dana's murder, but John thought otherwise. He knew that she was an accomplice to another recent murder. *The "other murder" is torturing her soul.* He debated interiorly if he should reveal his knowledge to her and concluded that charity demanded he address it later.

John looked at Jennifer standing alone, pitifully alone. She had no one except him and Allison. The recent headlines of the local newspaper set the town against her. At school, even most of her classmates shunned her. He knew that she received no support from her family, either.

He thought about the turmoil of Jennifer's soul, knowing she was alienated from God. If living in the fast lane wasn't enough, he knew she gravely violated her conscience as well. She suffered from an irreversible decision that went against every fiber of whom she was called to be.

John continued looking at Jennifer as she walked over to her nightstand to retrieve a Kleenex. She looked away from John as she wiped a small tear with a tissue. He suspected shame made her avoid looking in his direction. The sight of her crying alone was symbolic of her life. The worst part was that no one in this world cared if she was crying except for John.

John returned the letter to the dresser. "Do you know what a grace God is giving you at this moment? He told me to come immediately to your room and offer you hope. You were just about to take the pills, weren't you?"

Jen looked toward John and offered a faint smile. It wasn't an inviting smile but an expression to smooth an awkward situation. Her faint smile was followed with a nod yes.

John looked kindly at Jennifer. "God wants you to have hope, and He wouldn't have sent me here if He didn't have plans to help you out of this mess. Let me help you. I think I can free you from the mess you're in if you'll trust me."

"Free me from my mess? No way, it's too screwed up!"

"Give me nine days."

"Nine days!"

"I want to pray a nine-day novena to St. Jude Thaddeus." John grinned. "He's the patron saint for lost causes."

A genuine smile returned to Jennifer's face. *He makes me laugh.* She held no confidence in John's prayers, but she longed for his consoling presence even if it would be short lived. "I'll give you nine days. That's it."

John looked at the clock. "That means I have until 10 p.m. next Wednesday. If God could create the world in six days, then certainly St. Jude will be able to save you in nine."

Jennifer didn't find much humor in his last joke, probably because she didn't believe God created the world in six days or that St. Jude would be any help. Nonetheless, she felt comforted that John would be trying to help her.

John looked at Jennifer's purse and held out his hand. He gestured for the bottle of sleeping pills.

Jennifer sighed. She opened her purse and retrieved a full bottle. She put them in John's hand. "I want them back in nine days if you fail. Agreed?"

John knew he could never agree to such a request, so he replied, "Your questioning already suggests you don't believe in me. I thought you just agreed to trust me."

Jennifer held out her hand requesting the bottle back. When John hesitated, she added, "Trust *me.*"

John placed the bottle back into her hands. Jennifer walked into her bathroom and emptied the bottle in the toilet in plain sight of John. She flushed it and returned an empty bottle into his hands. She looked tearfully into his eyes, "I'm trusting you."

"I won't let you down," John promised. His eyes left hers and looked at her bedroom doorknob. An uneasy feeling came over him. "I think I need to leave now, but here is a prayer card I grabbed for you. Every time you doubt God loves you, read this card, even if you have to read it a hundred times a day."

After Jennifer closed the window, she stood silently looking out the window, contemplating how the events of the last ten minutes changed her life. It occurred to her that she might not have been alive at this moment had John not shown up. The uncertainty of what might lie after this life filled her with uncomfortable feelings of isolation and solitude. Upon hearing her bedroom door creak open, she turned around and noticed her mother standing at the door. "Mom, you have to knock before coming in here!" she objected.

"Are you planning on sneaking out of your window again?"

Jennifer turned around and faced her mom. "Do I look dressed to sneak out?"

Jennifer's mom looked at her nightgown and stopped her accusations. "Your dad wants to take you out for your birthday on Saturday. He said to take the train to the city and meet him at the Ritz-Carlton for lunch."

"My birthday is next Tuesday," Jennifer said.

Her mom ignored the correction. Both of them knew that Jennifer would be fitted into his work schedule whenever it was most convenient for him; any protest would be useless. "Be nice to him. When you two don't get along, he takes it out on me."

Jennifer lowered her eyes in submission. "I'll try." But she wondered if he would keep their appointment or postpone it like he had last year.

"He said that after he posted bond for you, he asked his lawyer to petition the courts for your custody. Your arrest is giving him the ammo he wants to make me out as an unfit mother."

"I'm sorry. I'd like to stay here near my friends if you don't mind."

"Fine with me."

Jennifer knew that neither parent really wanted her, but for some reason they sure spent a lot of time fighting over her. A smile formed on her face. "I know what I'd like for a birthday present."

"What's that?"

"A lock on my door."

"Do you think you deserve a lock on your door?"

"I'm endlessly interrogated by the police. All day at school I have to suffer cruel comments about being a murderer. Halloween coming up on Friday isn't helping. Then I head home to face you, who barges into my room. It would be nice to have just a little space in this world I could call my own, one that wouldn't be violated."

"Would you promise me that you wouldn't sneak out of your window if I gave you a door that locked?"

Jennifer put on a mischievous smile. "I've never lied to you, and I won't begin now. I can't make that promise, but I'll promise if you give me a lock, I'll always return."

Jennifer's mom didn't find any humor in her daughter's reply. A feeling of anxiety came over when it occurred to her that there might be some truth in Jennifer's subtle threat. "I'll think about it."

"Mom, this is one of those times I'd like to be alone."

Once she found herself alone in the room, she looked at John's prayer card. On the front, it had a beautiful young nun. The back of the prayer card read:

Jesus said: Let the greatest sinners place their trust in My mercy. They have the right before others to trust in the abyss of My mercy. My daughter, write about My mercy towards tormented souls. Souls that make an appeal to My mercy delight Me. To such souls I grant even more graces than asked. I cannot punish even the greatest sinner if he makes an appeal to my compassion, but on the contrary, I justify him in my unfathomable and inscrutable mercy.

– Saint Faustina Kowalska's diary, Divine Mercy in My Soul

Chapter 6

"Although it's a tight race, together we'll win for the children, for the moms, for the dads, for all citizens who make up this great state of Missouri!" Governor Wilson shouted into the microphone. He ended his rally with, "It's great to be home!" The crowd roared as he walked away from the podium to the edge of the stage. His wife, Margaret, and son, Peter, joined him on stage and waved cheerfully to the supporters.

John's mother, Mary Lightman, cheered from the section reserved for campaign volunteers. Governor Wilson passed through this section, waving and shaking the hands of his staff, before jumping into a limo with his family. Once they passed the last supporter, they rolled up the windows. Governor Wilson pushed the button to raise the dividing wall between the chauffer and the family. For added privacy, the stereo was turned on.

The cheerful smiles left their faces.

"Ten days of kissing babies is making me reconsider my pro-life position," joked the governor.

Margaret gave her husband a seething look. "Don't repeat that comment, Peter," she ordered.

"You can repeat it if the pro-choicers gain 10 points in the polls," teased the governor. He turned to Peter. "You mentioned last week that you had an emergency to discuss with me, and you didn't want to use the phone. I'm happy you used your discretion because just about all communications are being tapped nowadays."

Peter readjusted himself in his seat. "A week ago a girl showed me some very incriminating pictures," replied Peter, looking at the floor.

Governor Wilson was unsure if he wanted to continue this conversation but had no other option than to ask, "What type of incriminating pictures?"

"Of me, but I swear I have no idea where they came from."

"Have you been drinking again?"

"Not that much."

"How bad are the pictures?"

"Bad!"

"When you become a politician one day, you'll learn that to survive you always have to be putting out fires. How much does she want?"

"I don't know. I asked her, and she said let's wait till your dad gets back in town and then talk. She was in no rush to discuss business. It looked like she enjoyed watching me squirm."

"Where can we find her?"

"You'll need a shovel because she's six feet underground. Her name is Dana Keller!"

Governor Wilson threw his face into his hands and cried, "The teenage girl who was murdered about a week ago! When I told you over the phone to take care of whatever was wrong, I didn't mean that. What did you do?"

Chapter 7

"Must be nice having senior privileges," commented Jennifer as she and John walked through the school parking lot to his car during their lunch break on Tuesday.

"Next year you'll have the same privilege."

"I get a good feeling trusting that God told you we'd find a clue in Dana's dresser." Jennifer nervously joked, "Since we're skipping our lunch, I guess we'll be fasting for a successful break-in."

John grinned at her humor. She was in a rare good mood. *Does she know how special she is?* Suspecting Jennifer wouldn't do well in a high-stress situation, he thought it best to change the subject and keep it light. "You look a little tired. Didn't you sleep well last night?"

With a devilish smile, she said, "I would have slept much deeper if you didn't take away my pills."

"Not funny!" John face grew serious as he noticed Peter by the exit of the parking lot.

Jennifer picked up on John's concern. "I was just kidding."

"It wasn't that. Peter's handing out re-election flyers at the exit, and it might be best if he doesn't see us together."

"Are you embarrassed to be seen with me?"

Embarrassed to be seen with one of the prettiest, most popular girls in school? "Yes …" After a pregnant pause he continued, "I'd lose the esteem of Uncle Scott if I was associated with you."

A chill ran down Jennifer's back at the mention of Detective Peterson. She was reassured with the thought that if they got caught breaking into Dana's room, she would have John at her side. She replied with a polite smile, "I would hate to tarnish your altar boy image."

"Good!" He replied in jest as he opened the back seat car door. "Lay down on the floor seat, and I'll throw the blanket over you."

Jennifer complied. "Thanks for tucking me in."

He poked her side. "Be quiet."

She giggled anxiously.

John waved at the guard as he drove off campus. A block later, John said, "You can get up now."

"Yuck! You could have at least cleaned the floors."

John just smiled while keeping his eyes on the road. "Jennifer, I know I already told you, but I think I should break into Dana's on my own. You're already in enough trouble."

"Like it or not, you need me. I'm familiar with Dana's home, and you're not. Besides, I know the combo to the back door and won't give it to you. Just admit it, you need me!"

John thought it would be fruitless arguing so he replied with silence, but the anxiety of the present situation made it difficult for Jennifer to remain silent. "Since you're the most conscientious person I know, are we doing the right thing?"

"Since when did you begin to worry about doing the right thing?"

"What does that mean?" retorted Jennifer slightly agitated.

John didn't reply as he turned into Dana's neighborhood.

"You're right, I'm not really worried about doing the right thing, but I'm scared of getting caught."

"We can turn around."

"If I were alone, I'd chicken out, but with God on my side, I'm feeling confident."

"I hate to pop your bubble, but I'm not God."

"Yeah, but you're close to Him, so He'll look out for you. Since you heard in prayer to look into Dana's dresser, then God must be on our side." Jennifer looked into the visor mirror and checked her hair. "Aren't you scared?"

"Not really."

"Why?"

"Helping to prove your innocence is an act of charity on my part. Whatever happens, God will be pleased with my intention. One of God's attributes is that He is justice itself. He wants justice to reign on earth. It's a sad fact of life, but too often human justice is quite imperfect. He knows my intention is to only help prove your innocence."

Jennifer teased him. "Isn't there a commandment, 'Thou shall not break into thy neighbor's house'?"

"Our intention is not to break into Dana's home but to work for justice in regards to her murder. I've given this some thought and figured it would fall into the situation of the lesser of two evils. You might be falsely convicted of murder, which is a far greater evil than snooping around Dana's room looking for clues. So, although I'm reluctant to snoop around Dana's room, there are no other options."

Jennifer wasn't sure what to make of John's reasoning, but it really didn't concern her. She was grateful for his help; the moral ramifications didn't concern her. "We should park in this cul-de-sac and walk the last bit to her house."

Once the car was parked, the pair walked casually toward Dana's house. "We need to go around to the garage side door, which has the digital lock," instructed Jennifer. She nervously punched the numbers on the keypad. John looked in all directions to ensure no one was watching. Seconds later, they were tiptoeing across the living room floor. Jennifer almost had an "accident" when the cuckoo clock went off. John laughed hard at Jennifer's confession but managed to recompose himself.

The two proceeded to Dana's bedroom. Jennifer froze at the spot where she'd held Dana's corpse just a week earlier. She relived the emotions she felt, tears flowing. John held her for a moment and tried to comfort her.

"Why did God have to create death?" she asked.

Now isn't the time to answer such a complicated question. In an effort to deal with such a deep topic quickly, John asked, "Would you like to live forever?"

"What a horrible thought! Just last night I didn't even want to live 'til tomorrow." Jennifer reflected on John's logic that death would be far better than no death at all. *What a depressing thought to think that one would be sentenced to live forever on earth.*

"Is she in heaven?" Jennifer whispered.

John didn't reply.

"Is she in hell?"

Again, John didn't reply.

"Tell me then, how does God judge?"

"His Mercy and Justice are two sides of the same coin. He wants us to be His children more than we want it for ourselves. His perfect love doesn't impose, though, which leaves the soul free to chase all the empty pleasures of this world instead of Him. He patiently waits for us to turn toward him and to be recreated into His perfect image. The most important thing is for the soul to love God."

After a pause, John continued, "Have you ever told a lie?"

"Yes."

"Used His name in vain?"

"Yes."

"Gotten drunk?"

"Yes."

"Sinned against purity?"

"Yes."

"By your own admission, you've characterized yourself as a drunken, lying, blaspheming fornicator. If you were to stand before God, where do you think you'd be sent?"

Jennifer stared at the spot where she held Dana's dead body. She almost replied that she would be sent to where Dana went but decided against it. If John didn't want to judge Dana, she thought it would be best for her not to pass judgment as well. *Where would I be sent?* The answer she came up with embarrassed her, so she remained silent.

John allowed a couple of minutes to pass to permit the reality of what was said sink in. He took the pause in their conversation to look carefully around the room. There was an empty feeling—but something more than that, it was a cold feeling. An eerie sensation came over him. "I don't think we're alone. We'd better look in her dresser and get out of here."

John walked over to the dresser and opened the first drawer. He turned and noticed Jennifer standing there frozen. "What is it?"

"Maybe she didn't love God, but she didn't hate Him, either."

"Hate is not the opposite of love; indifference is."

Jennifer's heart pounded. John's answer troubled her. She felt convicted. If that was the case, she had a lot to be worried about.

"Jen, come on. Let's look through the dresser and get out of here," commanded John. He went through the drawers one at a time and found nothing. He turned around. Jennifer was stiff as a rod. John looked on the back of the dresser in vain.

He then noticed that the dresser had a base which could be accessed from the bottom drawer.

"What that's noise?" cried Jennifer as they both heard the garage door open.

"Stay calm. I just need to look under the bottom drawers."

Before he could do this, Jennifer bolted out the bedroom door. *She panicked!* He took out the bottom, left drawer but found nothing. He heard a man yell for Jennifer to stop. He replaced the left drawer and took out the right drawer. He saw a thick, leather diary hidden under the right drawer. John placed the diary under his sweater and carefully replaced the drawer.

He closed his eyes and prayed, "What now, Lord?"

He opened his eyes and noticed the bedroom window overlooking the front yard. He slid out the window and closed it behind him. His fingers started passing through the beads of his rosary as he casually strolled back to his car. Just upon entering his car, he noticed a police car, with blearing sirens, headed for Dana's house. He feared the worst for Jennifer as he drove away.

Chapter 8

The next day, the last school bell finally rang. The hallways were crowded with students scurrying to leave. John was putting away his books in his locker when he felt a gentle hug come from behind. Perfume filled the air. Uncomfortable with the situation, he said dryly without turning around, "Hi, Beth."

Jennifer let go and corrected him, "It's Jennifer!"

John turned, blushing as he looked at her.

"I'm so sorry for what I said earlier today. I've felt horrible all day. I truly didn't mean it when I said wished you were dead. Thanks for not laughing when Peter chimed in, 'Now you know what I had to deal with for six months.' My life is falling apart, and the stress is incredible. Our wild goose chase at Dana's house got me into a lot of trouble. My anger is always getting me into trouble. Please forgive me."

John had come to expect short bursts of anger from Jennifer. She'd been having them ever since the "other murder."

"We're friends, and sometimes these things happen. By the way, thanks for not telling the police that I broke into Dana's house with you."

"How did you know that I didn't tell them?"

"My uncle is Detective Scott Peterson, and if you dropped my name as being an accomplice, he would have shown up at my house last night."

Jennifer's face lit up. "Maybe if you talked with him, all this could get worked out."

"I tried a couple of days ago, but he won't listen. He's just doing his job."

"He could do it a little nicer."

John decided to change the subject. "Tell me what happened after you fled Dana's bedroom. I'm not sure which rumors to believe."

Her bad mood was beginning to surface again. "I'm glad you find my ruined life so entertaining!"

John didn't bite at her attempt to arouse pity from him and just smirked.

Flashbacks regarding Jennifer's recent arrest filled her mind. "I ran out the back. Mr. Keller ordered me to stop. I just ran and jumped the neighbor's fence. When I was halfway through their yard, a pit bull came running toward me. I climbed the nearest tree and waited for the police to show up. Mr. Keller was furious. I saw a side of him I've never seen before. At the police station, Detective Peterson drilled me into the evening. I never said one word. I just sat there quietly. The DA wants to delay my arraignment hearing a week because he believes the break-in might be related to the murder. At a minimum, they're going to charge me with unlawful break-in and attempted burglary."

The totality of the situation began to overwhelm Jennifer, and in a moment of weakness she snipped, "I should have just read my horoscopes rather than listen to your prayers."

That comment doesn't deserve a reply. John sighed.

Jennifer's conscience began gnawing at her, "Sorry. My emotions are on a roller coaster. I do respect your faith."

One moment she was the most compassionate, loving person you'd ever meet, and the next she was a roaring lion. Although those close to her struggled with her recent mood changes, John understood why she had them and was therefore a little more forgiving. "No apology needed. You've only made one error in our conversation this afternoon."

She could tell he was teasing but decided to play along. "Not pretending I was Beth?"

John shook his head. "That the break-in was a wild goose chase."

A gush of excitement came over Jennifer's face. "What did you find?"

"Oh, look at my watch. I'm late for snipe hunting. Let's chat over lunch tomorrow, and I'll tell you everything."

She playfully placed her hands on his throat and pretended to choke him. "Tell me what you know or you'll meet your maker!"

"Uncle," Peter shouted as he walked by, laughing.

I hate you! Jennifer gave Peter a seething look. She started to throw a book at him, but John grabbed her hand at the last moment. "If you throw that book at Peter, the judge will throw the book at you. Forget what he said. It's not worth getting angry over. I'll tell you what I found if you promise to remain calm."

Jennifer took a deep breath and agreed.

"I found Dana's diary."

"She talked about keeping a diary."

"I haven't read it, but I did notice that its last entry was the day before her death."

Jennifer became concerned regarding what Dana might have written about her. "May I have the dairy?"

"No. It doesn't seem right for you to read it."

"She dead!"

"Only her body is dead, but she still lives. We still need to respect her as a person. Since I didn't know her, it might be best if I read it."

Although Jennifer didn't want John to read it, she was at

a loss for an argument otherwise. So she sarcastically replied, "Why didn't I confide in someone with less scruples?"

"Someone with less scruples wouldn't have been enlightened by God to the diary in the first place."

Chapter 9

Governor Wilson stood motionless as he watched the rainfall from his library window. He wondered if the dead leaves on the ground symbolized his political life. Just yesterday, the last fall leaves were shining in the sun; whereas, today they were dead and decomposing.

His thoughts turned to his son. *Peter had so much hope. What happened to him?* He and his son were close. Peter idolized him, and maybe that was the problem.

Did he spend one too many nights away from home? Deep down he knew the place of a father was to be with his family. His own father had been a farmer, devoted to his family and, along with his wife of 60 years, considered the "salt of the earth" by others. Although Governor Wilson loved his family, he loved the life of a politician even more. His conscience always bothered him that 20 years ago he didn't move his family to the state capitol. How could he have known that the first election he won was only the beginning of a life-long career? The lives of powerful people are often filled with regrets, and his life was no exception.

Maybe a career-ending scandal would be good if it would allow him to be the dad he never was. He sighed that no matter what happened, there was a silver lining. Even so, he was determined not to relinquish his political career without putting up the fight of his life.

A knock at the governor's door forced him to end his reflections and deal with the problem at hand.

"Come in."

"Dad, Gene's here for the meeting."

"Good. Both of you come in and have a seat."

Gene Simpson, the campaign manager, walked into the room. He was a short, stout, round-bellied man who was never the life of a party. Everyone has a role to fill in society, and his was that of a political strategist. He knew just what buttons to push to gain the maximum amount of votes for a candidate. He was a modern mercenary, which meant he would fight on whatever side paid the most. In his thirty years of fighting dirty political battles, he never double-crossed a previous client, which earned him the respect of a trusted man, his only virtue.

"Gene, thank you for driving down on short notice."

"Governor, I'm here to serve you," he replied with false humility.

"I have to fly to the capitol in 20 minutes for a speech, so let's cut the formalities and get down to business. My son was being blackmailed and has a photo he doesn't want me to see, but I've talked him into letting you see it. Of course, I trust complete confidentiality."

"Of course," Gene responded matter-of-factly. He prided himself on his nickname, "The Fire Fighter," because his life was spent putting out fires that the political candidates started.

The governor turned to his son. "Peter, you can trust Gene. He'll guide you through this."

Peter took a deep breath and handed Gene a sealed envelope. Gene peaked at the photo and returned the picture back into the envelope. He closed his eyes in disbelief.

Governor Wilson wanted to know Gene's assessment. "How bad is it?"

"Both your careers are over if this comes out."

Gene handed the envelope back to Peter. "What do they want?"

"I believe there's only one girl who's part of the blackmail scandal. I believe she wanted money."

"What do you mean 'wanted' money?"

Peter replied sheepishly, "She's dead."

"How did she die?"

"She was stabbed to death about a week ago."

"Do the police have any suspects?"

"One suspect, Jennifer, the girl I used to date."

Gene knew not to ask any questions that might incriminate either him or the governor. So asking who actually killed the girl was a question he never would ask and, frankly, he didn't care. Too many men in his position ended up cleaning toilets in the "big house" for asking nosey questions, and he didn't want to be one of them. His job was damage control, not justice.

"Do you have any information that could link your old girlfriend to the murder?"

"Sure."

"Then by all means, be a good citizen and help the police."

Peter understood Gene's sly intentions. "My thoughts exactly! I've already been providing the police with evidence."

"Good job. This picture is probably a digital photograph. Where's the file?"

"I don't know. It must be on Dana's laptop or phone."

"It needs to be found and destroyed." Gene continued with a sense of indignation, "Peter, if you want to follow in your father's footsteps as a politician, then I would suggest you radically change your ways. This picture is completely unacceptable."

Peter protested his innocence. "I don't know where this photo came from."

"Peter, I wasn't born yesterday," responded Gene.

"Gene, I believe my son is telling you the truth," interjected Governor Wilson.

Gene looked at the governor. There was no use arguing the point since Peter was Jack's son, so he took another angle. "Eleanor, 'The Witch,' could sink to something like this."

"Who's Eleanor?" asked Peter.

The governor replied, "My opponent's campaign manager."

Gene decided to sum things up. "Governor, with only two weeks before the election, the timing couldn't be worse. The latest polls show the race is close. Don't see ghosts in the corners where there are none. Jack, you need to stay focused on the talking points and win this election. In the future, this matter will only be discussed between Peter and me. I think it would be best if you were out of the picture. If things go south, I'll be the fall guy, not you, understood?"

"Understood."

Chapter 10

After her British Literature class on Thursday, Jennifer joined John for lunch in the cafeteria. With the best old English accent she could offer, she began a conversation, "My lordship, thy maid beckons thy mercy. Soon I will be thrown into the gallows forever, but thither is hope my fate might changeth since I trusteth my life in thy hands."

John pondered a fitting reply. He held out his hand with his palm down. "My Lady hath entered the king's presence without kissing his ring, and thou wanteth mercy?"

Although Jennifer began to regret that she began this folly; nonetheless, she bent over and kissed his hand. *John paybacks are hell. You'll be sorry for this.*

John, still pretending he was a king, asked, "Why doeth thou believe thou deserveth mercy and not justice?"

"Because thy king is a God of Mercy and thou wouldn't wanteth to disappoint Him." Jennifer said triumphantly.

John smiled at her comeback. "Yes, my King is the King of Mercy, but He is also the King of Justice."

I have him on this one. "But justice is His to mitigate, not thine!"

John noticed Peter in the background watching. "Mercy shall be given on one condition."

I hope I don't regret this. "Thy wish is my command. Thy servant say'th yes before thou even asks."

"Then gaze thy eyes on thy king and no one else."

Jennifer teased him, "Will thou doeth the same?"

Looking down at his plate, John answered, "If I looketh at

thou, then it wouldst be hard for thy king to findeth the food on thy king's plate."

Jennifer smiled and continued to obediently look at him. "While I gaze at thee, I wondereth what thoust learned gazing at Dana's diary."

"Today, when the clock striketh four, we shall goeth to our rendezvous place and discuss the young maiden's diary."

"Thanketh thee." Jennifer began playing with her fork as she stared at him. "Did you ask me to stare at you because there was someone behind me that you didn't want me to see? Like Peter?"

"Yea," John ended his accent then continued. "Sometimes we should avoid looking at things that might make us sin. Temptations come in life, but we must try to avoid them if at all possible. It's not a sin to be tempted, though. Actually, it's meritorious when we fight temptations like dragons that need to be slain."

In a gentle and sincere tone, Jennifer asked, "Is that why you didn't want to enter my bedroom the other night?"

Her question went unanswered.

Chapter 11

At 4 p.m., John and Jennifer met at their favorite place in the park.

John said: "I needed to talk to you alone about the diary and a personal item. The cafeteria wasn't the right place. First, I need to say ever since the 'other murder,' I've noticed that you've been drinking a lot more and have been struggling with frequent bursts of anger."

Jennifer misunderstood him and tried to defend herself. "I've only gotten drunk once since Dana's murder, which was at her funeral." They both knew that her drinking episodes would have been greater if her mom didn't keep close tabs on her after the impending indictment by the police.

"I wasn't talking about Dana's murder but about your abortion."

Jennifer stood frozen. Her abortion was an unending nightmare. "How did you know? Was it in the diary?"

"I was praying at the abortion mill and saw you go in a month ago. I yelled for you to stop, but you never heard me. The diary confirmed my worst fears."

Jennifer appreciated there was not a tone of condemnation in his reply, even though he referred to it as a murder. "It's funny, in a sick way, that everyone believes I am a murderer. What I mean is just about everyone in school, the police, and even my parents believe I killed Dana. The ironic part is that I am a murderer, not in regards to killing Dana, but by killing my own unborn child. Life has become unbearable. I want this pain to be over, and that's why I almost committed suicide." Jennifer hid her face in her hands and cried.

Tears began swelling up in John's eyes. He knew that suicide rates skyrocket with post-abortive women. "Jennifer, your pain wouldn't be over if you committed suicide. It would just be beginning. I'm afraid your suffering would be much greater and without end, if you had taken your life the other night. Please go to the website called Silent No More. You're not alone. There's help for the guilt that is crushing you."

Jennifer looked away as the tears continued to fall. Her gesture made it obvious she didn't want to discuss her abortion with him. "Can we talk about the diary instead?"

Forcing the issue would not be productive, so he conceded to her wishes. "Last night, I read Dana's diary for the third time."

"Are there any clues to who killed her?"

"Yes."

"Great. Let's call Detective Peterson right now."

"I wouldn't suggest doing that."

"Why?"

"In the diary, I can see at least four people who could have committed the crime."

"Who?"

"Peter, Dana's dad, and someone she doesn't refer to by name."

Nervously, Jennifer inquired, "Who's the fourth?"

"You. I don't want this diary to become public for numerous reasons. If the police saw the diary, I fear it would be used against you."

John got out a clipboard, "Let's start with her dad. What do you know about him?"

"He runs a cattle and horse slaughtering operation. I think business has been good because Dana's family was never hurting for money. He could be a cheapskate when it came to spending money on Dana, though. She would cringe when folks complemented him on being a great father. I often asked her to talk to me more about her home life because her parents are divorced like mine, but she always refused. Her dad's a jerk, but I don't think he did it."

"How did Dana treat her dad?"

"Horribly! I don't know why. On numerous times he would walk into the room, and she would pretend he didn't exist. She wouldn't even acknowledge his entrance with a look."

"How about Dana's mom?"

"Dana's mom is a flight attendant, so she's not home much, which is why Dana lived with her dad. They seemed close even though they were so different."

"How so?"

"Her mom behaved like a professional career woman, and Dana was a wild teenager."

"A year ago, how often did you hang around Dana?"

"We might have talked a couple of times a month back then."

"Six months ago?"

"The same."

"Four months ago?"

"We started hanging out a lot more. We would get together or talk almost daily."

"Why the change?"

"I don't know, Dana just started hanging around me more. She told me that I was different than her other friends. I recall her characterizing her other friends as fakes."

"How did her friendship make you feel?"

"Special. She was always supportive of me and patiently listened to all my problems. She seemed so agreeable that I don't think we ever fought."

"When did Dana begin doing heroin?"

"Maybe four months ago."

"It's expensive. Where did she get the money?"

"I don't know?"

"Did you use with her?"

"No. I just drank."

"Did she hang out with you and Peter?"

"Yes."

"Tell me about Peter's dad."

"Typical politician. He's all smiles in front of the camera. The happy family image is just a facade. I got along with his dad pretty well. We would play tennis together."

"You were that close with the governor?"

"Yeah. The last couple of months that Peter and I dated, they treated me like part of the family."

"Tell me about Peter."

"Peter has high hopes of following his dad as a career politician. Although the money isn't bad, without a doubt both Peter and his dad love the power that comes with the job. Anyway, we dated for six months and enjoyed each other's company." A slight feeling of betrayal came over Jennifer. "But Peter turned into a jerk overnight. He broke up with me a couple of days before the murder. Out of the blue he told me that he was falling for Dana, but I don't think he had any motive to kill her. Why would you suspect him?"

John ignored her question. "What is his 'girl trophy case' about?"

"I don't know. He never mentioned it to me."

"It's a black box he keeps in his closet."

"Oh, that. He puts his personal memorabilia in it. He once told me that he saved all my poems there, but he never referred to it as a 'girl trophy case.' " Jennifer found that name disturbing. A sick feeling came across her abdomen as she thought of Peter putting her poems in a box he referred to as a "girl trophy case." *Peter, I hate you!*

"How close were you and Dana?"

"We became close friends."

"Were you aware that Peter and Dana went out a month ago? You were out of town at your grandpa's funeral."

"Sort of, they mentioned going to a movie." Although Jennifer knew John wouldn't reveal the contents of the diary to her, maybe she could get some insight on how Dana viewed their friendship. "A year ago you wrote me a letter and explained to me that a true friend desired the 'good' for the other. You described a friend as one who found joy in the happiness of another. After reading Dana's diary, would you say that Dana was a true friend?"

John just discreetly looked away.

Jennifer looked at him, trying to figure out his thoughts. If Dana had been a true friend, he would have said so, but since John never spoke ill of anyone, his silence answered her question. *If Dana wasn't a true friend to me, then what was she?*

Chapter 12

The idea that Dana was never a true friend occupied Jennifer's thoughts ever since her conversation with John the previous day. Sure, Dana started dating her boyfriend shortly before her murder, but John's silence disclosed there was something more to Dana's facade of being her friend … much more. This fabricated friendship, which had the appearance of being a true friendship, really bothered her. What would motivate Dana to behave that way?

Her thoughts drifted to a conversation with John over spring break. John argued that the mind needed to be formed in truth so that the heart could desire something truly good; therefore, the world needed the Catholic Church so that it could be rooted in truth. This seemed like nonsense to her since she believed her emotions should be the litmus test to judge an action. She found it strange that John was adamant that emotions couldn't be trusted. Jennifer recalled replying that actions alone speak for themselves.

John explained her error was because she witnessed the benefits of natural law. God designed a law in everyone's heart to provide certain safeguards which keep cultures from falling into complete degeneration. For example, he explained there were two qualities in people that tended to moderate the world to a better place, shame and honesty. Shame often impels one to avoid acting in a manner that would be perceived as base and vulgar. This fear of public disgrace tempers a person to behave better.

Then he expounded that people have a natural tendency toward honesty because people perceive honesty as something good and noble. Since deceit, the opposite of honesty, is regarded as disgraceful, shame and honesty work together to help temperate the world. But these two virtues alone, without the aid of truth reigning in the minds and love motivating the hearts, could only create a mediocre world at best.

Her thoughts drifted to Peter. Living in the limelight of the governor's family was enticing. Being part of the powerful family and the center of attention was intoxicating. The limo and helicopter rides were thrilling. On the exterior, she came across as a prized girlfriend whose actions seemed noble. She was amicable with others, silent with the press, warm to his parents, and devoted to Peter.

Jennifer knew that maintaining her newly acquired rise in social status came at a price. She was willing to pay the price for what she hoped to obtain, happiness. She felt like life was cheating her because she paid that heavy price and was able to only possess a mirage of happiness that didn't last very long. It occurred to her that if this was the best the world offered, this world didn't have much to offer.

Peter was patient in their relationship, to a point. As the two grew closer, he demanded more. Often her consent to his demands made her feel uncomfortable and at times shameful. She knew the thought of public shame did temperate Peter's true desires, just not completely. Her disordered desire to entice him in order to possess his love didn't help the situation. In reflection, she wondered if John was right, and her shame revealed she was breaking a "law" God placed in her heart.

It bothered her deeply when she noticed that her self-worth shrank each step she took up the social ladder with Peter. After the abortion, her feeling of self-worth reached a new low. A feeling of numbness overcame her and never went away. Since the relationship radically changed after the abortion, she wondered if Peter felt the same way. Neither brought up the subject, though, so she could only guess.

Deep down there was an unquenched desire in Jennifer to be loved by others, especially by Peter. Although she believed this desire to be loved was a good thing, John told her otherwise. At the time, she refused to believe John was right when he told her that her desire to *be* loved was rooted in her selfishness. Rather, John explained, she was called *to love*, which for John meant to desire what was truly good for the other. For John, eternal life was the greatest good to be wished on the other and not this world's passing pleasures. It was unthinkable to believe she got the whole meaning of existence completely wrong.

The thought of Dana's false friendship deeply repulsed her. She tried to avoid thinking about her relationship with Peter because it only fueled feelings of hate in her. Jennifer was honest enough to admit now that the most disgusting person in this world was herself.

As she reflected on many of her mistakes she made in the past, it occurred to her that allowing her emotions to be her decision maker was a mistake. These emotionally decided decisions only left her with regrets.

The self-serving intentions that ruled her life made her no different than Dana or Peter ... or maybe only by degree. This bothered her because she didn't want to be like them, but rather more like John. *How much better would my life be today if I let my decisions be rooted in truth like John does?*

After these recollections, Jennifer looked up from her lunch plate. "I need help."

Misunderstanding her plea, John jumped in. "I heard you would be indicted next week and will go on trial in a couple of weeks. There's still plenty of time to solve this mystery. Remember I have five more days."

"That's not what I mean. I need help. I look at you and see how strong, patient, and loving you are, and I want to be like you. I hate myself most of the time."

"I can try."

Allison unexpectedly joined the two at the table. She ignored John and said mischievously to Jennifer, "It's Friday night. I'll come by your bedroom window at 11 p.m. Sneak out and I'll have a great surprise for you. We haven't partied since the funeral. I'll have some 'special lemonade.' "

"Can I bring John with me?"

Allison took one look at John and said, "He's a nice guy, but this isn't his type of party. We're going to meet four of the guys from the football team at the levee, but as of right now, there are only three girls. This is our regular group, and we want you to come."

"I'd rather hang out with John tonight. You could join us."

"You're lame," Allison replied, rolling her eyes as she stomped away from the table.

John and Jennifer continued eating in silence.

John took his last bite. "I guess we have a date. Since I know your mom still holds a grudge against my family, I'll park down the street from your house. I'll be there about nine."

Before she could object, he was gone.

Chapter 13

John leaned against his car breathing in the sharp night air as he waited for Jennifer to show up. He was glad to see the full moon because a little natural light would be helpful for the task at hand. Instead of idly waiting, he closed his eyes and pondered on aspects of God. Since his time was being put to good use, it didn't bother him that Jennifer was late.

Jennifer tiptoed up to him and contemplated his serene disposition. She whispered, "Hi."

He teased her by replying, "My maid, thou have kept thy king waiting. I could have thy head for this!"

She joined the folly. "My lordship, I fear thou will have to wait in line for my head. Thy uncle wants it, and if my mom catches me, she will want it as well."

John continued, "Ah, my lady, then hurry and tell how I can enter into Peter's castle so thou can escape such a terrible fate. I must look in the box before the moon reach'eth the midnight hour."

"Then thou need my lady to show thou the key and the box buried in Sir Peter's closet."

"Captains have the stars to navigate, pirates have maps, but I only need thy word to be on my way. Then my lady can lie'th peacefully on her bed instead of on the guillotine."

"How can I lie'th peacefully on my bed when thou wander uncharted waters? I fear thy boat will wander aimlessly like a ship without a keel."

"The battlefield is no place for a young, pretty maid to wander."

He called me pretty, that's a first. "To wander, no; to guide, yes. I'd rather die a hundred deaths than see my king flounder around with my fate at hand. I goeth with thou or I goeth alone, but I will goeth!"

John figured fighting her about staying at home would be a losing battle so he opened the passenger door. "My lady."

As Jennifer took her seat she pondered John's rich sense of humor. *Why is he so quiet and shy in school?* She wondered whether he had verbal follies like this with Beth or if this was something special they shared.

Driving away Jennifer asked, "What's the plan?"

"I just followed Peter to a keg party on the other side of town. I suspect he'll be there for a while."

"At least 'til 2 a.m."

"That's what I thought. His parents are back on the campaign trail so the house should be empty. How do we get in?"

"They hide a key on the back porch. Why do you need to look in the box?"

"Dana wrote that she put a surprise in his black box for him to find, but she didn't say what it was. This entry in her diary was just days before her death. From what was written, it was something very big. Often she wrote in riddles. I think it would be best if I only look in the box."

"Okay."

"Did Dana know where the key was?"

Jennifer thought a second. "Yes. She was there when he accessed the key a couple of times. Turn here; you can park in the driveway of that vacant house. Peter's house backs up to it."

The two quietly exited the car. With no street lights, the neighborhood was fairly dark. Large trees swayed back and forth, creating moving shadows on the ground. The area was full of high-income "McMansions" on large yards that breathed a feeling of isolation and eeriness.

John whispered, "Jennifer, look up. See the clouds rush across the sky as the moon is desperately trying to peak through. It looks like a scene from a scary movie, doesn't it?"

"Not funny. Unless you plan on holding me, I wouldn't make any more comments like that."

John held his tongue as he smiled in the dark of the night.

They slowly entered Peter's yard. They looked at his large, dimly lit house sitting off in the distance. The house was pitch black inside, and there was no sign of life in it.

Every step they took crumbled leaves and small sticks under their feet. Crickets chirped loudly. A barking dog from the neighboring house startled them both. The sound of a passing car made them stop and look back.

John commented casually, "It's amazing how many sounds you hear at night when you're petrified."

Speaking between clenched teeth, Jennifer replied, "John, *please!*"

John smiled again unnoticed.

The two took a couple of more steps, and John got a bad feeling about continuing. He decided it was best to keep his fallible opinions to himself, though. He reminded himself that his gut feelings weren't always right. He hoped that this was one of those times.

They reached the back porch. Jennifer removed the hidden key located on the underside of the deck railing and opened the basement door. They peeked into the large, pitch-black basement room.

Jennifer stood at the threshold shaking. "Peter's room is

just across the recreation room in the corner. Put your hand on my shoulder. I'll guide you."

John complied without saying a word. The two begin their journey across the dark room.

They didn't even take two steps when Jennifer bumped into a table, making a lamp fall over.

John joked, "You're no Helen Keller!"

Jennifer nervously returned the lamp to the table and with a tone of regret voiced, "I knew I shouldn't have brought you along."

"My thoughts exactly!" joked John. He pulled out his pen light and said, "Follow me."

Moments later they found themselves entering Peter's bedroom. Just as John returned the bedroom door to its closed position, they heard an upstairs door slam follow by the sound of heavy footsteps running down the basement stairs!

A look of terror came across Jennifer's face as John tried to assess the situation.

Chapter 14

As they stood in Peter's moonlit bedroom, they listened to the footsteps growing louder. John's attention turned to Jennifer as he sensed she was about to panic. He grabbed her hand to calm her down. He briefly closed his eyes to pray. He prayed a short prayer to himself, "Lord, guide me."

Jennifer felt a little more at ease feeling John's hand hold hers. She looked at him and an expression of complete disbelief overtook her face when she noticed his eyes were closed. *Tell me that this is just a bad dream and he really isn't praying!* She tugged him to the right and said, "Here, let's hide in the bathroom."

John opened his eyes and forcibly pulled her to the door on the left of the bathroom and said, "No, in here."

Jennifer complied without a fight and added, "That's his closet."

They hustled into Peter's large walk-in closet and shut the door behind them. They then quickly buried themselves in a pile of dirty laundry in the back corner. The pile of clothes must have been two feet high and were thrown under a stuffed closet of hanging clothes. As they positioned the pile of dirty clothes over their bodies, they heard Peter's bedroom door slam open and footsteps running for the bathroom.

Jennifer and John sat with their backs leaning against the bathroom wall. John considered the situation and knew there was nothing else to do but quietly wait. He whispered, "Everything is okay … don't panic."

Jennifer nodded nervously while John placed a trench coat over the top of their heads. He gestured to Jennifer to pull her legs up so that they were out of the closet's aisle. John instinctively grabbed his rosary and began praying interiorly.

They heard the toilet lid open followed by the sound of a man heaving his dinner.

John turned his head and softly whispered into Jennifer's ear, "I think Peter's worshiping the porcelain god tonight."

Although Jennifer was shocked that he would make a joke at a time like this, she did find herself anxiously smiling. "Some of his friends had the flu today. I guess he got the bug."

The toilet flushed and Peter was heard exiting the bathroom. Country music was turned on at a low-decibel level.

Next, the closet door opened and a light turned on. No one entered, though. Jennifer began to claw her hands into John's arm.

John softly whispered into her ear, "You need to find a new coping mechanism because your present one is killing my arm."

Jennifer was horrified that he made another joke now that the closet light was on. The joke only made her fear increase, causing her nails to dig deeper into his arm. John wasn't typically one to cry, but tears of pain started welling up in his eyes. Her response worked because greatly regretting his last comment, John had no interest in cracking another joke.

Peter entered the closet.

Peeking from the underside of the trench coat, John could tell Peter was right in front of them. He was relieved to notice that Peter's feet were perpendicular to them, which would imply he didn't notice them, at least not yet. He heard a drawer open and the sound of Peter changing. John breathed calmly knowing they hadn't been noticed and all would be fine. He felt sorry for Jennifer because she was not in a position to assess the situation and had to sit waiting in fear. Moments later, the closet door closed and the light turned off.

The two sat there in the dark with only the sound of music lightly playing in the bedroom. Jennifer was grateful for the music because it would afford her the opportunity to talk. Since silence wasn't her forte, she hoped a conversation would calm her nerves.

John felt Jennifer's hand move to rest on his chest. He quickly removed it and quietly asked, "What are you doing?"

"How come my heart is pounding with fear and you're as cool as a cucumber?"

John grinned and decided not to mention that he could tell by the position of Peter's feet that Peter hadn't discovered them. *She thinks I'm a man of steel.* He decided to take the opportunity to talk to her about fear. "Pardon the pun, but I fear my answer will bore you."

"There are no atheists in fox holes," Jennifer whispered in a tone of sincerity. "Please try me."

The sincerity in her tone compelled him to comply. "I studied a lot of philosophy at the minor seminary. There are different types of fear. Since we live in different worlds, we experience different fears. But all fear is born in love because man fears the loss of what he loves.

In your world, one has many fears. Although the most common is the fear of human respect, your fear tonight is rooted in what might happen to your person. To some degree your fear tonight might be rational; however, without the support of faith, it can easily become irrational. Because love of one's self reigns in your world, the preservation of self becomes one of your highest desires. People without faith will go against their nature and even kill for self-preservation. This, in turn, makes personal suffering your greatest enemy."

Jennifer quietly took in what he said.

John stretched his neck. "In my world, a person would fear losing the one he loves the most, which is God. Transforming one's thoughts, words, and deeds in a manner pleasing to Him is of the utmost concern. When this is done, concern of self disappears. As a person draws closer to the Lord, he'll cease to see much value in his own greatness or things of this world. Rather, he is motivated to glorify God. Consequently, since he is not focused on himself, the fear of punishment or suffering decreases dramatically."

After a brief pause waiting for her reply, John whispered, "Did I put you to sleep?"

Jennifer contemplated John's message. "No, I'm just taking in what you said. What you shared is very deep. Your schooling over the past two years must have been profound. I find it fascinating how you can describe what makes people tick. Is fear related to why I get angry easily?"

"To be honest, I don't focus on your shortcomings but rather try to see the good in you."

You're too kind! "I give you permission to focus on my faults and help me figure out my anger. Please."

"Give me a minute."

Jennifer leaned her head against the wall while she waited for his answer. Being in John's company gave her a feeling of security. She began to relax. Her head began swaying as she lip sang the Keith Urban song playing in Peter's room. *John Cougar, John Deere, John 3:16.*

A couple of minutes passed before John replied. "Here's your answer. You have a strong passion to love that which you find good and valuable. Your capacity to love is stronger than most, which is a great gift. You find pleasure and joy when you possess the good you love, like your relationships with people. When you see what you love being threatened, you get angry."

"You make it sound like my anger is good."

"It would be only if what you love is truly worthy of your love. In addition, your anger will manifest itself because something worthy of your love was destroyed."

Was that a reference to my abortion?

Again, footsteps could be heard hustling to the bathroom. The commode was just on the other side of the wall, so prudence demanded that they again observe silence. Jennifer welcomed Peter's gross interruption because it afforded her the opportunity to reply to John with silence.

Jennifer knew the answer. Her relationship with Peter and his powerful family fueled her ego with a sense of importance and self-worth. She loved to be esteemed by others. False love trapped her into seeking illicit pleasures of this world. Knowing that others envied her climb up the social ladder gave her a high. It was apparent that all her passions in life were rooted in self-love.

There was no doubt that Jennifer loved herself as the highest good in the world, but she wasn't ready to confess this to John. She presumed that her admission wasn't needed because she suspected he already knew.

John's reply also made her understand that her recent anger might be rooted in her abortion. This was a connection she didn't make until now. Deep down she knew her unborn child was worthy of her love, and she hated the part of her that destroyed her child. How to solve this anger still eluded her. She hoped over time the guilt would just go away, but it didn't.

Jennifer's thoughts drifted to why she enjoyed John's company. He wasn't good for her ego, nor did he flatter her like her others did. To be in his presence meant that she would have to behave differently, better.

It occurred to Jennifer that at this moment, she didn't long to be at the levee getting drunk. She, therefore, concluded that she was attracted to something or someone truly good and valuable. Although her life still seemed like a puzzle, she felt like for the first time in her life she was able to put some of the pieces together.

She again pondered on who Beth was but didn't know how to bring up the subject with John. *Was she pretty? How much did John like her? Why didn't he ever mention Beth to her in the past?* Maybe the biggest question Jennifer wanted answered was why she even cared about Beth since she liked John only as a friend.

Peter returned to his bedroom, which offered Jennifer the opportunity to continue the conversation but with the hope of figuring out John better. She whispered, "What you say seems to make sense. Since you have me figured out, allow me to try to figure you out by asking some questions. Your highest love is God?"

"Correct."

"You fear that you might lose him."

"Yes, but it's a different type of fear than yours. My fear is like a son not wanting to disappoint a father."

"I don't really understand that type of fear because I couldn't care less if I disappointed my dad."

John wanted to correct her disposition regarding her father but thought another time would be better. "Would you ever want to be good so as not to disappoint me?"

Jennifer turned her head toward him. "Yes."

"And me for you as well. I'd rather die than share the things you've shared with me in confidence. This conviction of mine is rooted in love for you, based on the fear of not wanting to hurt you."

"I get it now. Your fear seems nobler than mine."

"Yes, it's nobler because it is ordered in love." John continued, "Most people today have other false loves in addition to self-love. They might love pleasures, money, power, whatever. Regardless of the false love the soul embraces, all false loves leave the soul not fearing that they are offending God. God created us not to love ourselves but to be like Him, which demands we seek to love others, but Him first."

"I heard God is perfect mercy. So won't we all end up in heaven anyway? Why make a big deal out of it?"

"He is perfect Mercy, but He's perfect Justice, too. If someone prefers to cultivate his heart to false loves, when that person dies, he'll be given exactly what his heart wanted, which is not heaven with God. Jesus doesn't impose. A person filled with self-love would hate being in His presence so His Mercy allows that soul to descend to hell for all eternity."

"But, most people just go through life without ever choosing. It makes judgement so unfair."

"God gives everyone graces for salvation. I suspect some people respond to His grace and don't fully know it. Too often, though, we reject God's graces without even thinking twice. Deep down, we know there's a God, but most people choose not to seek Him. If we truly sought Him, we'd have His promise that we would find Him. When we die, we'll see clearly all the graces He gave us. Trust me, when your body returns to dust, you won't believe He was unfair wherever you end up."

"You see things so differently than anyone else I know. You've given me a lot to think over!"

"If I'm right and there's a God who will judge every thought, word, and deed, then only a fool would continue living his life like it didn't matter."

"Do you love anything other than God?"

"Sure."

"Like what?"

"I love my future wife. I make all my decisions in a way that would be pleasing to her. This world is a landmine for impure thoughts, so I'm on constant watch to guard them so as to please her. My total love for her compels my eyes to gaze at things which won't corrupt my heart. Every day, I fight the onslaught of temptations that could harm my future family. On my wedding night, I'll be able to present myself as a pure and noble husband worthy of her love. I do all this because I love her deeply."

The feeling of sitting next to the most thoughtful young man she'd ever met began to overwhelm her. His love for his future wife stirred Jennifer in a new way. Allowing herself to be caught up in her emotions at that moment, she replied in a wistful voice, "That was the most beautiful thing I ever heard."

After a couple of minutes, Jennifer's curiosity got the best of her. She just blurted in a whisper, "So who is Beth?"

"Just a girl who wants to change me."

"What does she want to change about you?"

John decided to tease Jennifer again. "She thinks I shouldn't hang out with girls who are drunks and murderers!"

Jennifer let out an unexpected burst of laughter. John threw his hand over her mouth, but it was too late. Jennifer laugh was at an unacceptable level for remaining hidden. All they could do was wait quietly to see if they'd be discovered. After a couple of minutes of waiting for Peter to burst through the door, they breathed a little easier, suspecting that he hadn't heard them.

The fear of almost being discovered changed their moods. Neither felt like talking anymore.

"I think I'm going to pray a rosary now. Why don't you try to rest because it will be a while before Peter is in a deep sleep."

"I'd like to pray with you. Will you teach me?"

John handed her his rosary, and he guided her fingers from bead to bead as he prayed. After a decade or so of instruction, he told her that it would be best for them to continue on their own in silence since Peter's music was now turned off.

◆ ◆ ◆

Three hours later, John firmly placed his hand over Jennifer's mouth and woke her up. Once she was awake and understood to be quiet, he lifted his hand from her face. John told her that his mission has been accomplished, and it was time to go. He helped her up and told her to follow him.

Peter's closet door squeaked as John opened it. He poked his head into Peter's bedroom, which was barely illuminated by the moonlight. Peter was snoring. John grabbed Jennifer's hand and the two quietly tiptoed through the room. Once they exited, John used his pen light on the way to the porch door and then his car.

"What did you find?"

"A very incriminating picture of Peter." John noticed Jennifer looked a little uneasy, so he added, "the picture had nothing to do with you."

Thank God. "I can't believe I laughed so hard when you said that Beth told you not to 'spend too much time with drunks and murderers.' At school I'm getting teased every day about being a murderer. I hate it. With Halloween just days away, I don't know how many people have asked me if I'm going to dress up as ax-murderer. Why is it that these murderer comments infuriate me, but when you said it, I burst out in laughter?"

"Because you know I'm a true friend." John answered.

My only true friend. "I do want to seek the good for you like you taught me a true friend would want to do for the other. I have a confession. Part of me thinks that I'm a good friend to you, and part of me thinks I'm selfish at times in our friendship. When I find myself using you, just in the smallest things, I hate myself, but I do it anyway."

"You need God's help if you want to love perfectly." John responded as he turned into her neighborhood.

Jennifer smiled. "That's the best reason to become Christian I've ever heard. Why don't you let me off here, and I'll walk the rest of the way."

John pulled the car over. Jennifer's house was located two doors down from where he parked. "You're back home safe and sound."

"Everything goes well when I'm with you," Jennifer added with a tone of sincerity.

John corrected her by replying, "I got you arrested at Dana's house."

"I got arrested because I left your side."

John decided not to respond to her comment.

Jennifer took a deep breath as she remembered the evening. She knew it was time to go and decided to express a gesture of gratitude before departing. "I would have never dreamed that hiding under Peter's dirty laundry would be one of the most memorable and wonderful dates that I can remember. Thank you!"

"It wasn't a date," John protested.

"Oh, yes it was. At lunch you said 'I guess we have a date at nine,'" Jennifer insisted playfully.

"That is not what I meant," replied John dryly.

"It doesn't matter how you meant it; that's how I took it," teased Jennifer.

After a long pause John inquired why Jennifer wasn't leaving, "Is there something else?"

Jennifer could tell John was uncomfortable with implying that they just enjoyed a date. She, on the other hand, was enjoying paying him back finally for him making her kiss his hand at school, so she continued, "I'm waiting for my kiss goodnight. That's expected protocol after a date, you know."

"I hate to disappoint you, but I'm saving my first kiss for my wife."

She replied seriously, "Really?!"

"Really!"

He is special. Jennifer started opening the passenger door. Another thought entered in her mind, and she couldn't resist sharing. Just as she was about to shut the car door she added, "Don't worry, I won't tell Beth."

John mumbled softly between his teeth, "I wish you would."

A big smile came across Jennifer face as she replied excitedly, "I heard that!"

Chapter 15

Jennifer was happy to be back in John's company; his presence was enough to change her whole outlook on life and make her troubles seem small, as if he took on her crosses for her. Otherwise, it seemed like the world was crushing her down from all sides.

Less than a day had passed since John dropped her off after Peter's closet debacle. Since many of those hours were spent asleep, their separation seemed small. Part of her hoped that he would not solve the murder case too soon or else she would lose his daily presence.

Their destination was a surprise to Jennifer. John only mentioned that he was going to take her to a gathering at a friend's house. Although Jennifer voiced concern about going out in public, John reassured her that his friends would not make murder jokes.

As John pulled his car into the Glenforks neighborhood, it became apparent to Jennifer that the destination was her old friend's house. Jill and Jennifer were best friends until their split a year earlier. Jennifer was anxious about being there but tried to make the best of it. It occurred to her that John was unaware of her contentious relationship with Jill because he was away during that chapter in her life.

Jennifer walked into the house alone as John excused himself to check on something near the car.

"Hi, Jill!" Jennifer smiled nervously. "Sorry for crashing your party. John brought me, but I didn't know where we were going until he turned into your neighborhood."

A warm welcoming expression came over Jill's face. "Jennifer! What a pleasant surprise to see you here. Can I get you something to drink?" *I mean non-alcoholic!*

The two smiled at each other over the question, thinking back to their sophomore year. Jennifer knew Jill was just trying to be polite, but given their past, her question had unintended implications, which created an awkwardness that they both found humorous. "A glass of water would be great."

"Come with me into the kitchen. There's a cooler you can choose a bottle from."

The two made it through the crowded room. Jennifer smiled shyly at the dozens of faces she passed. Although the greetings were warm, it was awkward walking through a party in which she didn't know anyone. She knew the group was composed of the town's interfaith Christian youth group, which wasn't her circle of friends.

Jill handed Jennifer a glass of water. "Let's go into the sunroom and chat. It will be less crowded."

The two walked into a cozy nook off the kitchen, which was surrounded on three sides by windows. The view of the lake was spectacular.

Jennifer was relieved to see that it was unoccupied. "This was always my favorite room in your house."

Jill sat down on the couch. "It's my favorite room, too. I've been really worried about you."

Jennifer took a nervous sip of coconut Vitamin water. "Thanks." She heard a noise and smiled at Jill's dog. "Come here, Snoopy! You were a bad dog. You should have let Jill in."

Jill laughed questioning, "What are you talking about?"

Jennifer was comforted that Jill would laugh in her presence. It had been almost a year since they laughed together. "I guess you were too drunk to remember, but the last night we were together you asked Snoopy to open the door for you. It was quite comical. I practically carried you home that night; you were leaning on me so heavily. When we reached your house, you couldn't find your key so you softly knocked at your front door whispering, 'Snoopy, let me in'. I kept telling you that Snoopy was a dog and couldn't open the door. You said he could. We went back and forth debating the issue. Then you said, 'Just watch. He'll open the door.' "

Jill hid her face laughing. "I was that bad?"

"Yeah. It gets better. Just then, the door started opening. I was dumbstruck. For a moment, I thought Snoopy actually opened the door for you." Jennifer laughed and shook her head in disbelief that she actually thought for a moment that Jill's dog opened the door. "Then I looked up and saw your mom staring at me. I'll never forget that look of disapproval. I have a confession to make. I let go of you and ran. I can still hear the thud your body made when it landed on the threshold."

Once Jill collected herself from almost uncontrolled laughter, she replied, "You're forgiven." Then adding in a more serious tone, "but really, I'm the one who needs to ask for your forgiveness. After rehab, I needed to run from my old life, which included you. In hindsight, our friendship deserved a better good-bye than the cold shoulder I gave you. I was weak, and I needed to get away from all temptations."

"You seem happy now."

"I am."

"Then I'm happy for you."

"Are you doing okay? I wish Peter was there to comfort you at Dana's funeral."

"We broke up several days before her death."

"I heard."

An indifferent look came over Jennifer's face. "He started dating Dana a couple of days before her murder."

"No matter how hard I try to avoid the gossip at school, I still hear it. So, it is true that Peter left you for Dana?"

"It's more complicated than that." Jennifer looked away, hoping Jill would catch the hint and change the subject.

I shouldn't have brought up Dana's death. "It always is." Jill ran her hand through her hair. "When my boyfriend dumped me two months ago, I felt really down. I had one of those moments. I walked out on the dock with my phone. Do you know whose number I started to text?"

Jennifer turned her gaze back toward Jill but didn't answer.

Jill smiled. "Yours!"

Jennifer was shocked. "Really? Why?"

"Part of me wanted to get drunk with you to relieve the pain. I remembered how you were there for me when my first boyfriend broke up with me two years ago. I'll never forget. I cried for hours on your shoulder."

"You'd better be careful how loud you talk. Some of your new friends might hear how you wanted to get drunk with me."

"Just because I'm going to church and in the youth group now doesn't mean I'm not tempted. The difference is now I have the grace to do what is right."

"I'm glad you didn't call me because you're a better person now than when we hung out."

"You know what I did instead? I put a picture of the two of us on the refrigerator. Every day since, I looked at the picture and thanked God for the good things we did together, like collecting cans for the food drive at school and helping Mr. Walker when he was on crutches."

"Thank you. You made my night."

"It gets easier over time to do what's right. At the beginning the temptations are relentless and seem overpowering. In time, by God's grace, they're less frequent and weaker." Jill reached over and put her hand on Jennifer's hand. "I'm glad you're here tonight and not out with your friends."

"Me, too." Jennifer looked down at her feet. "You left me when my parents were finalizing their divorce. I was an emotional wreck. In the midst of everything, I destroyed all of my pictures of us. Maybe you could copy a picture of us together so that I can put it on my dresser."

"Sure."

A look of horror came across Jennifer's face as she looked through the sunroom windows into the living room. "Is that your mom in the living room? Since when did you have parties when your folks were home?"

Jill grinned at Jennifer's comment. "She normally hangs out in her bedroom when I have friends over, but I guess she needed to get something. She'll be okay with you here."

I'm not going to find out! "Would it be okay for me to walk to the dock tonight? I'm not up for much socializing. A little quiet time would be nice."

Jill raised her eyebrows. "Sure, but the old bottle of vodka isn't under the wooden plank anymore."

Jennifer looked toward the living room and noticed Jill's mom was still occupied, chatting. Jennifer joked, "Did you drink it?"

Jill bit her lower lip. "Don't cry, but I poured it out into the lake."

"You used to say that was the unforgivable sin."

Jill sighed. "Yes, I used to say that."

Jennifer noticed Jill's mom heading for the kitchen. "Please tell John I took a walk to the lake, and I'll be back soon. Thanks."

◆ ◆ ◆

Faint moonlight guided Jennifer to the water's edge, and she enjoyed the soothing sound of ripples bumping into the long dock. An occasional stirring of leaves on shore could be heard, along with crickets. Jennifer welcomed the feeling of isolation.

At the sound of dry leaves crunching under footsteps, Jennifer asked, "Who's there?"

John appeared in the moonlight. "Me. Are you all right?"

"Yes, why wouldn't I be?"

Should I tell her? "When I heard you were gone, I thought that maybe you didn't want to be around Jill."

Jennifer gave John a peaceful smile. "I had a good talk with Jill. Although she's from an old chapter in my life, I'm so glad we had a chance to talk. I think we got closure on what happened last year. Even though I'm not ready to be close friends with her again, I do feel comfortable going back to the party in a couple of minutes and chatting with her some more."

John looked back at the house, which could barely be seen through a patch of trees. "How close were you two?"

"Besties! It's hard to believe that it's been almost a year since she stopped hanging out with me. Our relationship grew when you were at boarding school. This dock brings back a lot of memories. I think I could just sit here all night dreaming about all the good times I had on this lake."

John didn't respond. His eyes traveled down the shore line in front of him.

Jennifer continued, "I can't wait until this nightmare of mine is over. It would be nice going back to how life was before the divorce. I'm tempted to live with my father so that I could switch schools. A fresh start might help."

John stared through the woods that separated them and the house. He again offered no reply.

What is he thinking? I guess he doesn't want to talk about my life tonight. "In Jill's living room, I met a girl named Beth. She didn't look thrilled to meet me. Is she the Beth you mentioned?"

Sheepishly, John replied, "Bingo."

"She's cute."

"But she's not my type."

"How about Jill? I can give you a good reference. She's beautiful and unattached now. Want me to put in a good word in for you?"

John laughed. "Jill and I have worked closely together running the youth group. Over the past two months, we've become close friends. She's not my type, either, and I'm not hers."

"Why not?"

"Our faith is the most important thing to each of us, but we express it differently. I'm a Catholic and she's a Protestant, so we have significant differences in our beliefs. She can be a great friend but not a future prospect. It's hard for you to understand from your world."

"Are there any attractive Catholic girls at the party?"

"Four."

"Give me a name. I'll mingle in the crowd, and let me see what happens. I'm really good at this. I used to do this for Jill all the time."

Rubbing his eyes in frustration, John replied, "Why do you want to do this?"

"You've been so kind to me, and I'd like to return the favor. I thought if I could match you up with the perfect girl, I could make you happy."

John glanced at Jennifer. "Thanks for the kind gesture, but I'm in a good place right now. We see things so differently that we'll have to agree to disagree on what makes someone happy."

When Jennifer looked up at him, she noticed his gaze toward the shore. "I've been thinking about the things you shared with me last night. Your insight into my false loves was right on. Will you please explain the contrast between your ideas of happiness and mine?"

John hesitated for a moment. "Okay. Honestly answer this question. If you were with Allison right now, what do you think you'd be doing?"

Honestly! "Because I'm trying to change, I think I'd have told Allison a dozen times that I didn't want to drink with her, but after a while, I would have given in because there's nothing else to do in this small town. By the end of the night, I'd probably be pretty toasted. Sorry, I know that's not the answer you wanted."

"It's exactly the answer I wanted because it's the truth. I would have been disappointed if you said anything else."

"I don't get it. What does your question have to do with being happy?"

John looked compassionately into Jennifer's eyes. "You're suffering immensely, and you'll do anything to escape it. Last week, you fantasized on how our camping trip from hell was what heaven will be like."

They both giggled.

John continued. "Tonight your mind is wondering back to getting drunk with Jill. You think switching schools might make you happy. You've confessed that if you were with your friends right now, you'd be getting drunk. Often your heart longs for the past or hopes in the future. You believe you'll find peace by escaping the present moment, like drinking or suicide."

"And you?"

"I believe a person can only find happiness in the present moment. God is only in the present moment, so it's only there one can find true peace."

"Why don't you try to walk in my shoes? If you were falsely accused of murder and only one person believed in your innocence, how would you maintain peace?"

"I don't pretend to have that great of faith, but I know the answer. I'd remind myself that God knows the truth. I would listen to the voice in me, which has been formed in the truth, and try to always do what's right. If I could do that, then, by the grace of God, I would have peace."

"You make it sound so simple."

"It is simple, but it can be hard. The alternative, which you try to live, is much harder and sometimes impossible."

Jennifer considered his reply. Then she decided to ask him about a question gnawing at her all week. "How can I find peace with my abortion on my conscience?"

"If you had to do things differently, would you?"

"Actually, I wish I would have followed the path that you took three years ago after the campout."

"My path took me to a different world."

"Yes, I mean I would have taken your path of faith but also your commitment to chastity. I wish I could live for my future husband like you live for your future wife. You didn't answer my question, though. How can I find peace given the crime I committed?"

"It takes faith to see your soul like God does. God is in the present moment. It appears that you have the requirements of a sincere confession." John looked kindly into Jennifer's eyes. "I can assure you that He is looking at you this moment with such tenderness that you would melt if you could feel it. There is no greater joy He would feel than to let Him transform you into a beautiful daughter of God. You need to seek true love and happiness."

Jennifer tilted her head back to look at the immense heaven above her and not allow John to see the mist in her eyes. "Thank you."

"You're going to hear voices, sometimes from others, sometimes within your head, telling you otherwise. You must recognize that they're lies and not believe them. Don't forget, do what is right and be at peace. If you do this, you'll remain a precious child of God. This is just the first step in your walk with God. We'll talk about the next step later."

"I spent a few hours reading Silent No More's website over the past days, after doing my homework. I feel a fire burning within me to defend life. Part of me is wondering if these feelings are because I'm not trusting in God's forgiveness and need to do something to make up for what I've done."

"No, that's the voice of God speaking to your heart to atone for the wrong you've done. Since God put it there, you're going to have to listen to it to have peace as well. Throughout life, God will put opportunities in front of you to be a voice for the unborn. Welcome them as opportunities to honor your child."

"I'm scared, but deep down I know you're right."

"You're on the right path, Jen. How about going to church with me tomorrow?"

"I'd like that, but Mom won't be up until late morning. She

says it's her only day to sleep in. I'll need her permission before leaving the house. Ever since my arrest, she's been keeping me on a short chain. "

"Problem solved! I talked to her when you were getting ready and asked if I could take you to church. She already said yes. Also, I asked her to come along, too, but she declined. Was she okay tonight? She seemed to be acting weird."

"It's Saturday night, you know, date night. She's very lonely and every Saturday night she goes to the bar."

"I'm sorry."

"It's not fair because Dad is not lonely tonight."

"It's not all his fault."

"Yes, it is."

"At the campout our families went on, he wanted to take your family to church on Sunday but your mom ridiculed him in front of everyone. She got a couple of extra hours of sleep while my family went to church. She wanted a godless husband, and she got one."

"I know a lot of godless husbands who are decent family men."

"Hmm, I wouldn't say there are a lot. Remember what I said last night? Everyone will have to choose whether to live for true love or the false loves of the world. Your father needed your mother's support to make the right decisions but didn't get it. Believe it or not, he's suffering, too. You, especially, should know not to believe the facade of worldly pleasures."

"I guess you're right. So the other woman and drinking are the way that he escapes his pain. I'm starting to get it. Things are beginning to make more sense. How should I view him?"

"Just pity him and show him that you love him. Fill your thoughts with the good things he does."

The two heard a noise at the other end of the dock. John instinctively flipped open his hunting knife. The darkness of the night afforded little opportunity to correctly assess the situation.

Jennifer looked at John in disbelief. "You carry a knife?"

"Please be quiet. I heard something."

The two sat in silence for a minute while they listened for further noises. Nothing else out of the ordinary was heard. John returned the knife into his right pocket. "It must have been just a tree branch falling. It's a little cold out here. Let's return to the party so you can finish your conversation with Jill."

As the two got up, Jennifer decided to tease him. "Do you really want to return to the party so that I can chat with Jill, or do you have an ulterior motive like flirting with a Catholic girl?"

"That question, Nancy Drew, you'll have to figure out all on your own! Ladies first."

Jennifer smiled. *I'll try.*

Off the dock, the two walked in silence back to the well-lit house. Unknown to Jennifer, John had again pulled out his knife and kept looking from side to side. Once on the back porch, he discreetly returned the knife to his pocket. The living room in front of them was crowded with people too preoccupied to notice their return.

Jennifer stopped before the glass door. She looked pensive.

John took the opportunity to open the door for her. "Madam."

Jennifer ignored the polite gesture and firmly re-shut the door. "I have a question for you. I noticed that some of the girls here dress 'hot.' I know you're not attracted to girls who dress like that. Are any of the four Catholic girls at this party dressed that way?"

John dropped his head. "Yes, all the Catholic girls here are dressed 'hot,' as you put it."

Great! I have no competition. "You jerk!" Jennifer had to bite her tongue to keep a serious disposition.

John was stunned by her comment. "I'm sorry, you lost me."

I'm going to make him squirm for his Nancy Drew comment. Pretending to be offended, Jennifer continued, "You jerk! I know all about guys like you. Over the past 20 minutes you basically confessed that inside this door is a party full of attractive Christian girls, but not one of them is good enough for you. I should just go in there and announce your high-horse piety to all the young ladies present."

John remained calm as he deduced her ploy. *You almost got me flustered. How would you like it if I turn the tables?* "I noticed that you made that assumption while standing outside the house. Let me open the door so that you can test that assumption standing inside the house."

John reopened the door.

Don't say you're attracted to me. It's too soon for that. I might revert to my old ways and hurt you. But, on the other hand, John please don't tease me and still say no girl in this room would interest you, I would be crushed. Jennifer took one step in the house and turned around. Looking at John warmly, she replied confidently, "I don't have to ask that question because I think I already know the answer."

Jennifer left him there standing alone to ponder her reply.

John watched Jennifer walk away and disappear into the crowd. *I wonder what she thinks my answer would have been because I'm still unsure what I would have said if she called my bluff.*

For the next hour, John socialized with old friends. From the corner of his eye, he kept tabs on Jennifer just in case she decided to take another walk alone.

As he maneuvered into the kitchen, he was disappointed to see Jennifer talking to Kelly. Jill stood uncomfortably beside her.

Jennifer waved her hand in disbelief. "That's a lie. It's not the woman's body to do with it as she pleases. Look at a picture of an aborted baby; the arms and legs ripped apart are not the woman's. They're a child's!"

Kelly began fuming. "It's not a life but a fetus. If you were a little more scientific and less emotional, you'd see the truth."

Jennifer remained calm but determined to fight. "Fetus means 'little one' in Latin. That's a good term to use because he or she is a little human. By the time of the average abortion, this little one has its own heartbeat, its own DNA, finger prints, nose, mouth, tongue …"

"I get the point." Kelly shouted as she interrupted Jennifer. "Personally, I wouldn't have an abortion, but I believe it's a woman's right to choose."

"Why not just allow rape under the guise that it's a man's choice?"

"That's a ludicrous argument! Rape is a crime that violates the rights of another person."

"Abortion deprives the right to life from the unborn baby, and it does it in a brutal and traumatic way. Ultrasounds show unborn babies fighting for their life during the procedure, and 'scientifically' we know they feel the pain."

Kelly could tell she was losing the debate. "But often it's the best answer for the woman and the child. Everyone wants to reduce unwanted pregnancies and child abuse."

Jennifer shook her head in disbelief. "Abortion is child abuse. Abortion goes contrary to the nature of what it means to be a woman. Most women need to be coerced in some way to choose it. I was coerced by those around me to have an abortion. I was told that abortion would be an eraser, but it didn't erase anything. It felt like I did the most awful thing imaginable, to pay someone to kill my child. No one told me the unexplainable emptiness I'd feel. I've been plagued with dejection, agony, anger, nightmares, and thoughts of suicide. Abortion is murder and needs to be rejected by all elements of society."

Kelly laughed sarcastically. "You have a corner on this murder thing then, don't you?"

Jennifer dropped her head and closed her eyes. She repeated to herself, *I did what was right, I can be at peace.*

Jill hugged Jennifer and whispered, "I didn't know. I'm so sorry."

When their embrace was released, Jennifer put on a fake smile. "I'm glad we had a chance to talk about our old friendship, but I think it's time for me to leave now."

Jill sighed. "Let me walk you out."

Passing John at the kitchen doorway, Jennifer said softy, "I'll be waiting in the car whenever you're ready to go."

John nodded his head. "Just a couple of minutes."

As the two girls entered the empty foyer, Jill broke the silence. "I think everyone one in the kitchen, especially me, was grateful for how you handled Kelly. All of us have tried to get her to see her views on abortion are wrong but to no avail."

Jennifer paused at the front door and stared outside. "Thanks."

"Maybe we could sit on the dock someday and catch up."

Jennifer reached for the door knob. "I need some time to get my life together. Call me next summer, and I'd love to come by."

Eight months from now?! Jill was disappointed but said, "I understand. Good night."

Jill walked to the front door and watched Jennifer walk away. *John, why did you park your car on my front lawn instead of the street?!*

John entered the foyer and pressed the unlock button on his key chain. He gently moved Jill from the doorway and positioned her against the wall to the left side of the door. He, in turn, took her place looking out of the front door to ensure Jennifer's safe arrival to his car.

Jill pushed her head back against the wall and closed her eyes. "I wonder if we should allow Kelly to stay in the group."

After John saw Jennifer enter his car, he quipped, "Kelly can perfect you better than I can."

Jill smiled at his reasoning. After a brief silence, Jill continued, "I'm glad you brought Jennifer tonight."

"Me, too. So what are your plans for tomorrow?"

Jill turned and looked at John and noticed he didn't return the glance. "Church at nine, brunch at Lisa's, and then the park. A group of us are meeting there. Rumor has it that a new guy's interested in me. Why do you ask?"

John briefly looked at Jill, who was now staring at her guests through the foyer hallway. "I need a favor."

"Sure. I'm free after four."

"I was hoping from ten on."

Jill sighed her displeasure at his request, "Involving Jennifer?"

"Yes." John answered without emotion.

"Jennifer was polite but distant to me. She made it clear we're no longer friends. I don't think I'm the one for your mission."

"If you're there, trust me she would welcome you as a friend."

Jill's eyes studied John's face to understand his plan. "Your mom dropped by the flower shop this morning when I was working. She said you got in at 2 a.m. this morning and wondered if there was something with the youth group going on last night that she didn't know about. She was going to ask you, but apparently you slept in late today. Were you out with Jennifer last night?

John continued staring outside. "Yes, but it's not what you might be thinking."

John, why are you acting like this? "I'm trying not to judge you, but you're making it very hard. You know you've become one of my best friends. Given how much I care for you, I need to tell you that your recent behavior is worrying me. During our entire conversation, you've stared non-stop at Jennifer. For some reason, you decided to park in my front yard, which my dad will be furious to know when he sees the lawn in the morning. Then you share with me that you had a late night with her. John, Jennifer's one of the most enchanting people you would ever meet, but she's not good for you, at least not right now."

John continued to look at his car. "I'm not obsessed with her. I just need to ensure she's safe."

Jill rolled her eyes. "This neighborhood isn't quite the inner city."

"On the way here, I noticed someone following us, so I looped around the library all the way to the post office before entering your neighborhood. A white Ford Explorer followed us the whole way. I parked in the yard so that we'd have a short walk to the door. Tell your dad I'm sorry."

"Must have been someone from out-of-town because anyone else would have noticed your detour didn't make sense."

"My thoughts exactly. Once I escorted Jennifer into your house, I sneaked around to see who our 'friend' was. I noticed the driver briefly talked with Nick and Jane as they were walking in. The Explorer turned around and stopped at your mailbox for a moment before departing. I asked Nick, and he said some guy was looking for the Cooper birthday party off this street. The driver asked a couple of questions about this party and left."

"I've lived on this street my whole life, and there's no Cooper family."

"I suspected as much."

"Does Jennifer know someone followed you here?"

"No. I thought she needed a peaceful evening, so I kept it to myself. I'll tell her on the car ride home."

I wish she would have found my home peaceful. "She can stay here with me tonight."

"I told her mom I'd have her home by eleven, even though Jennifer said her mom would be at a bar."

"Why do you think someone would want to follow her?"

"I'm not sure she was the one being followed. I might be the person they want."

Jill giggled as she replied, "John, you're a good Catholic boy. Why would you be followed?"

"Just between you and me?"

"You can trust me."

You're one of the only girls I know who can be trusted with a secret. "Dana was brutally murdered for knowing too much information regarding a couple of individuals. I know everything she knew, which puts me at risk."

Jill became elated. "So Jennifer didn't kill Dana?"

"No, she didn't."

Jill demanded, "You need to go to your uncle with this."

"I tried and he said, 'murder weapon, motive, confession, case closed. Please leave, I'm busy.' "

"Your uncle is like that. I guess Jennifer knows too much, too."

"No. I've kept a lot of the details from Jennifer, but Dana's murderer doesn't know this."

"So you want me to babysit her tomorrow?"

"I wish that was the case. Tomorrow after church, I'll have to tell her that her new best friend was using her. Dana was a drug addict. She was being paid to pretend to be Jennifer's friend to get dirt on the governor's family. When Jennifer became pregnant, Dana was paid a huge bonus if she talked Jennifer into an abortion to create a public reelection scandal for the governor."

"Why would Dana do something so evil?"

"It wasn't the old Dana, but the new Dana addicted to drugs. They just took her over." John's eyes turned to Jill. "Anyway, I know I've been spending too much alone time with Jen. It's not my place to be there for her after I tell her, but I sure wish she wouldn't have to be alone. Maybe it's what God wants. Nevertheless, I'll only be there for a short time and then I'll go."

"What about asking your mom to be with Jennifer?"

"She'd be perfect, but she flew out of town this afternoon and won't be back until late Monday."

Jill shook John by the shoulders. "Look at me. I cannot believe what you plan on doing. You can't tell Jennifer that a boogey man is following her around and then drop her off alone at home. And if that isn't enough, you're going to tell her tomorrow 'by the way, your close friend wasn't a friend at all but had her unborn child sacrificed to buy a couple more votes for an election!'"

"I have to tell her about the boogey man out there so that she takes more precautions. And Dana's diary will be public news soon enough, so it's essential that she hears this news from me and not from a newspaper." John stared in the distance as he collected his thoughts. "She's placed all her trust in me, and I feel that I'd betray that trust if I kept this a secret from her. I wish it could be kept from Jennifer for the rest of her life, but it can't. The next best thing I can do is be the one to tell her. Everyone close to her has betrayed her—her parents, her boyfriend, and Dana."

Jill added, "Why not just say her old best friend, Jill, betrayed her as well?"

"I wasn't thinking that."

"It's true. I let her down, too. I wonder if I'd done things differently, if she would have done things differently." Jill looked up and noticed her mom approaching the foyer. "Mom, I need a favor. Please host my party. I need to help Jennifer out tonight and hang out with her tomorrow."

Jill's mom tensed up. "What do you mean, 'help Jennifer'?"

"I haven't had a drink in eleven months. Trust me; I have no plans on breaking my record tonight."

"That's not why I'm worried about you, honey!"

Oh my gosh, she thinks Jennifer is going to stab me! Jill responded sarcastically, "Don't worry, I'll hide the kitchen knives."

John turned and looked at Jill in disbelief.

Jill threw her hands in her face and blushed. Whispering toward John, "I can't believe I just said that."

John smiled. "Don't worry. If Jennifer were here, she would have been the first to laugh."

"Really!"

John nodded yes.

"I miss her so much."

Chapter 16

Monday afternoon at school, Allison swiped her lunch card after filling a plate and started looking around for a place to sit. She noticed Jennifer sitting in the back corner alone. She wondered why John wasn't sitting with her but was glad. She'd have an opportunity to apologize.

"Hi, can I join you?" Allison asked cheerfully.

"Since when did you need to ask if you can join me for lunch?" replied Jennifer kindly.

"Since I was a jerk last Friday and called you 'lame.' I'm sorry."

"It's okay."

"What's this about the police showing up at school today?"

"Apparently, there was a break-in at Dana's house last night, and Detective Peterson wanted to question me."

"You didn't break in again!"

"No. I had an airtight alibi. I was at home with my mom."

"Did the detective believe you?"

"Do you believe me?"

"Should I?"

Disgusted, Jennifer gave Allison an unbelieving look and decided to change the subject. "So how did the levee party go?"

Allison sighed, "Not good. Jim turned into a mean drunk, and the fourth girl we invited threw up all over the place including in my car. Saturday, I had a horrible hangover. I don't know why I do it ... So how did hanging out with John go?"

Jennifer closed her eyes and took a deep breath. "It was wonderful!"

"You're kidding."

Jennifer leaned forward and whispered girl talk, "Even worse. I asked him for a kiss, and he said no."

"Why does he hang around you?"

"He said it's for charitable reasons," added Jennifer to goad Allison on.

Allison laughed so hard that her last sip of soda exited her mouth and found a resting place in her napkin. "Girlfriend, you've got a bad case of the rebound blues. Listen to yourself. You went from dating the governor's son, who looks like an Abercrombie & Fitch model and is in a powerful political family, to dating a guy who won't kiss you and only hangs around you because he considers you an act of charity. I wouldn't trade my Friday night horror for yours any day of the week."

After a moment of silence, Allison realized something. "You like this guy, don't you?"

"A lot."

"Does he like you?"

"I don't know. John and I have been friends for years. Recently I'm seeing a different part of him that I like. He treats me differently than the other boys, and I like it." Jennifer took a sip of water as she collected her thoughts. "We're in different worlds, though. I'm trying to change so that he looks at me differently."

"Shouldn't he accept you for the way you are?" asked Allison.

"Why? I don't think I like me, why should I ask him to? Oh, here he comes. Change the subject and be nice."

As John was approaching the table, Jennifer asked, "Hey, John, sit here."

"Ladies."

"Hi, John," replied Allison as she sized him up. He was no

less handsome than Peter but dressed more casually, in Dockers and a plaid flannel shirt, not trying to draw attention or give the impression that he overspent on clothing.

"So what are you two talking about?"

The girls looked at their food and quickly took bites. Jennifer's fork beat Allison's to the task at hand, so Allison felt compelled to reply. "Jennifer was just commenting on how she has to change to get the things she wants in life."

John looked puzzled as he closed his eyes to say grace.

Jennifer took advantage of John's distraction to give Allison a disapproving look.

Allison smiled and opened her note book.

Wanting to change the subject, Jennifer asked Allison, "What are you studying?"

"My Shakespeare class. Romeo and Juliet. I failed miserably in my last analysis of Macbeth, and I'm struggling to come up with something meaningful about this play. All I can come up with is it's a play of love and the willingness to die for the other." Then in a melodramatic tone she ends with, "The older generation family feuds just got in the way of true love." Allison returned to her normal voice and said, "I think this insight will give me a C- when I really need an A." Turning to Jennifer she concluded, "Any thoughts?"

Jennifer pondered Allison's question. "I'm sorry, but what you said is basically what I wrote in my analysis last year. And I only got a C." Her eyes turned to John. She stared at him to try to get his attention, but he didn't return a glance. "John, what are your thoughts regarding Romeo and Juliet?"

Allison suspected his answer would be a waste of time.

John looked up at the two girls. "Romeo and Juliet is not a love story. The physical realities they experience are symbolic to represent the spiritual realities that Shakespeare was trying to express. A romantic interpretation of the book is wrong because the age of romanticism didn't enter Western literature until 200 years after the play was written. Modern people are blind in their own fallen ideas to see the truth of the story.

To Shakespeare, true love demanded the virtues of discretion and self-restraint. Neither Romeo nor Juliet had either of these virtues. True love is to be a gift of self to the other. Both Romeo and Juliet's loves were not for the true good of the other, but for pleasures and love of self. Romeo's motives are an antithesis of true love because he takes what he knows isn't right for him to have, her innocence. He's a rebel against the natural order of man and that of God.

Juliet is a young, immature, thirteen-year-old girl whom Romeo convinces to let untamed passions rule in her. She behaves rashly and with no virtue. Shakespeare calls Juliet a holy shrine of innocence, which Romeo's only desire is to desecrate. It's not about love but lust. Lust is a sin they choose to commit together, which leads them to mutual destruction. Shakespeare expected the reader to know that their physical deaths are nothing more than a symbol of the spiritual death they willingly chose when they first kissed. Because they sinned together, it's only fitting that they share despair and destruction together."

John stood up. "Excuse me while I get seconds."

Allison was speechless. "Whoa, that was brilliant! Where does he get that stuff?"

"I told you, he's in a different world. He sees things differently from us. He paid attention in his philosophy classes at his old school, too."

"How come we couldn't see it?"

"I think we might be a bunch of Juliets," joked Jennifer.

A couple of minutes later John returned and inquired, "Where did Allison go?"

Jennifer pushed her empty tray to the side. "To prepare her Shakespeare report before she forgets your amazing reply."

John gave Jennifer a doubtful look.

"I'm serious!" Jennifer, then, put on a playful smile, "Your uncle dropped by school to see me today."

John was surprised. "Why would he do that?"

"He dropped by to follow up on a tip he received last week. He asked me if I placed my hand on your throat and said, 'Tell me what you know or you'll meet your maker!'"

"How'd you reply?"

"I thought about how someone in your world would reply. So I decided to tell the truth. Also, I didn't want to focus on trying to defend myself. I said 'yes.'"

John closed his eyes and took a deep breath. "I think you need a little more catechizing. I'll straighten out the chokehold comment later today with him. Was that all he wanted?"

"He said he heard we were now dating and wondered if that was true. She bit her tongue in order to keep a straight face as she continued, "I don't think Peter told him that we were dating. Was it you?"

John decided to tease her back, "Maybe, so how did you answer?"

Jennifer giggled at his quick comeback. "I just said, 'We're not dating. John considers being with me an act of charity.'"

John was astonished at how her interaction with his uncle didn't frazzle her. Instead, she seemed at peace. *What a contrast to your conversations with Detective Peterson last week.* "You're in great spirits today. Why?"

"It's thanks to you I keep repeating in my mind what you

said about God looking down on me with love. Don't laugh, but I asked Jill to repeat those words to me as well, which helped me get through Sunday."

"I'm glad Jill was there for you."

"Me, too. I couldn't have made it without her. We talked for a couple of hours after you dropped us off Saturday night." Jennifer started giggling.

"What's so funny?"

"I'm just thinking of all the boogeyman jokes and stories we made up. I laughed so hard."

"Someday I'd like to hear them."

What she was about to share deeply moved her. "Knowing I was too scared to sleep, Jill put a chair by my bed and told me we could take shifts sleeping while the other stood guard. I fell asleep first. Jill said I slept restlessly. Sometime in the middle of the night, I briefly woke up and noticed her still sitting there beside the bed. She told me to sleep a little longer. The next thing I knew it was seven in the morning, and she was still sitting there drinking a cup of coffee."

John took his last bite of lunch. "Jill told me that you took the news I told you on Sunday well. I'm proud of you!"

Jennifer smiled at the mention of Jill's name. "Please don't make me out to be a saint because I really wanted to drown my sorrow in one of Mom's liquor bottles. The temptation to get drunk was very strong. After you left, I cried. The anger I felt was overwhelming. Did Jill tell you I went to the liquor cabinet?"

John shook his head no.

Thank you Jill. "We were sitting at my kitchen table and talked for hours. About two hours after you left, I mixed a drink and brought it to my lips. I asked Jill if she was going to stop me and she replied, 'No. I just shared with you my thoughts on why you shouldn't get drunk. I won't say anything else, and, to tell you the truth, if you get drunk right now, I promise I'll only think good thoughts of you. I regret abandoning you once when you needed me, and I won't do it again. Whether you're drunk or sober, I'll be here for you.'"

John finished his last bite. "She is special."

Jennifer nodded yes. "Then she closed her eyes. I don't know if she was praying or if she closed them so that I wouldn't feel bad drinking in front of her. I took a sip, but before I swallowed it I noticed a tear run down her cheek, so I spit it out in the sink and asked what was wrong."

She replied, "I hoped abandoning my guests for you last night and the sacrifice I made by staying up all night by your bedside would be enough to show you how much I love you. It was my hope that you wouldn't discard my love for a bottle."

"So what happened?"

"I recalled that you said a person should forget about himself and focus on others. So I gave it a try. I put away the bottle and suggested we take a walk in the park. Although I didn't see the Explorer in my lane, I wasn't going to take a chance. We sneaked out the back door, jumped the neighbor's fence, and ran to the park."

"She had plans at the park."

"She didn't tell me, but when we got to the park, we found some of her friends there. We hung out most of the day with them. There was a new guy there who took an interest in Jill. I hung around this new guy and Jill just long enough to help them break the ice. As soon as I saw that he and Jill were comfortable talking, I left them for the volleyball game.

"I bet Jill appreciated what you did."

"She thanked me on the way home."

John noticed Jennifer playing with her fork. *She wants to ask me something.* John patiently waited.

"How do I know that this faith thing isn't just a crutch for those who need it? I've repeated those words you've told me probably a thousand times since Saturday night. It gives me peace, but what if it's all just a mind game?"

"You're asking the age-old question. There are many ways I could answer that question, but for you, I'm going to offer a very personal reply. Do you believe in Jill's and my love for you?"

"Yes."

"When you have doubts, think of our real love for you, knowing that it's actually the love of God working through us. You can believe in our love for you because you can see it."

"But, Jill could fail me again."

"She's a different person than she was a year ago. Better. Although it would be sad if she failed you again, you still have the memory of her love for you right now to give you hope."

"Part of me wants to keep my distance from her, and part of me wants to forgive her."

"You know the better part of you wants to forgive her."

"I know."

"Here's the deal God wants to make with each of us. He knows we live in a broken world, which has a lot of toes being stepped on all the time, including His toes. He's willing to forgive us provided we forgive others."

"So I need to forgive her?"

"Yes, along with forgiving Peter and Dana."

"I might forgive Jill, but Peter and Dana are another story." Jennifer wanted this conversation to end. She reached over and grabbed John's hand. "John, you've dropped some bombshells on me recently. Don't let my happy disposition and smiles fool you. Internally, I'm barely making it, and I doubt I could handle anymore right now. Could we have this conversation some other time?"

John grinned. "Okay, you're right."

Chapter 17

Later that day, Jennifer was at the park sitting at her favorite place feeding the ducks when John approached.

"It's not like you to keep me waiting. I started wondering if you got my text." Jennifer decided to try to make him feel a little guilty. "Since now I know you got it, I feel a little cheap waiting here for the past twenty minutes for you to show up."

John sat down on the park bench, unmoved by her comment. "I had a last-minute distraction." He turned to her and replied in jest, "You're not impatient like Juliet was, are you?"

"No!" *Please don't compare me to Juliet.* "But it just doesn't seem proper for a gentleman to make a girl wait alone in the park."

"You weren't alone. Why did you ask me to meet you today?"

What does he mean I wasn't alone? If I ask him, he'll probably say God was with me. "I'd like you to tell me more about what you know about who murdered Dana and why. Being left in the dark on these details is really starting to bother me."

"Okay, but I'm going to bring up subjects that you're not going to like."

Like what? "I can handle it."

"Where do you want to start?"

"I want to know the motives of the three people who could have killed Dana. Why would Dana's dad want to kill her?"

"It seems as though she was attempting to blackmail him. She spied on him and discovered some illegal activity he's up to."

"Why would she want to blackmail her own dad?"

"Dana needed to fund her heroin addiction. Every addict

will steal from their family, and Dana tried it through extortion. The addiction just takes over a person. She started becoming desperate for money."

"Why would Peter want to kill her? They'd just started dating."

"As I told you yesterday, Dana befriended you so that she could get some incriminating information on Peter's family and ruin his dad's chances for re-election. She insisted that Peter pay for the abortion and took an incriminating picture of him, too. It also looks like she had thoughts on blackmailing him for money."

"What can you tell me about this mystery person who might have killed Dana?"

"Dana only used derogatory names when referring to her in the diary. This woman is politically powerful and dedicates her life to the 'cause.' I believe it has to do with abortion."

"Is that all you know about the fourth person?"

"From what I discovered, this woman was paying Dana to come up with some scandalous stuff on the governor. This person seems to be powerful and evil."

"Why would she want to kill Dana?"

"Just before her death, Dana double-crossed her."

Jennifer gained the courage to ask him the question she was dying to know. "You've had about a week to study Dana's diary. Who do you think had the greatest motive to kill her?"

"You had the biggest motive." John said matter-of-factly.

Jennifer wished she didn't ask that question. She didn't want to know his reasons why the diary would put her on the suspect list. She could think up a half of dozen reasons why right off the bat. If there were more, she had little interest in knowing them.

"I need just a few more pieces of the puzzle to put this together. I'm really close to setting you free. I still have two days left. The next couple of days are going to be busy for us. Trust me, the end is near."

"I trust you." Jennifer added in all sincerity.

In a teasing tone John asked, "Did you know you have a secret admirer?"

Is it you? Jennifer ran her hands through her long curly hair and looked into John's eyes. "And who might he be?"

John gently set both his hands on each side of her head and leaned his head in close to hers. From a distance, it might have given the appearance that they were lovers. His gentle grip turned into a firm one. "Don't turn around, but I noticed a guy followed you out of the school parking lot. He's been standing behind the stone chimney at the pavilion staring at you the whole time. When I saw you were safe waiting here, I doubled back and found his Ford Explorer in the school parking lot. It seems like he's been following you and not me. I'll ask my uncle to run his plates to see who he is. I'm going to let you go, but promise me you won't turn around."

Jennifer nodded yes.

John removed the firm grip he had on her head. "Let's walk out the west entrance of the park, and as soon as we get behind the bank, we'll run the back alley to your house."

"So he's after me and not you."

"It appears that it's your lucky day!" John looked at her modest attire, which she wore for him. "At least today you're not dressed to kill for!"

Jennifer kiddingly seethed. "God can't be love if he sent *you* to help me!"

Chapter 18

The next day, the school bell rang at the end of another school day. Jennifer found John putting away his books in his locker. His daily routine made him easy to find.

Jennifer approached John from the rear. Instead of a typical hug, she placed her hands on his shoulders and laid her head on his back. She thought he would probably appreciate this "modest" hug instead.

John felt the intrusion of hands on his shoulder. He recognized Jennifer's fragrant perfume. With a smile on his face, he replied without turning around, "Hi, Beth."

Jennifer couldn't believe her ears! With a playful burst of anger, she hit him across the back.

Pretending he made an honest mistake, he replied melodramatically, "Oh, I'm sorry. It's you Jennifer."

Jennifer stared at him. "You knew it was me, you jerk!" she playfully teased.

John just grinned, again enjoying her company.

"Hey, in a couple of minutes I have to leave for a meeting with my attorney and the DA," Jennifer replied with a slight tone of anxiety.

"Relax, I'm sure they just want to wish you happy birthday."

"I wish. It's a plea bargain session."

John pulled out a piece of paper. "I wrote down my last unsolved riddle from Dana's diary. I've been able to decipher all of her riddles except this one. I thought maybe you could try to help me figure it out. It reads:

Oh, Sorceress who feeds me with stardust
You serve a master who is the prince of this earth,
Oh, Sorceress promises yours truly so many things my heart delights,
Who can bring snow in July is a friend to behold!
Leunam, Leunam, Leunam is my backward snowman,
If diamonds can be found in ruffs, then snow can be found in dung,
Paternal secrets provide the key to power and control.

Handing her the riddle, John finished with, "Take it home and try to figure it out. Let me know what you come up with."

"All right. Oh, Detective Peterson pulled me out of class today to ask me some more questions. This makes two days in a row visiting me. Apparently, someone tried to break into Dana's house last night, and they wanted to know if I had anything to do with it."

"Where were you last night?" he asked in a suspicious and almost accusing tone.

Jennifer pretended to be astonished at his insinuation. "I didn't do it!" She then changed her tone and asked inquisitively, "Was it you?"

"No. How dare you suggest it was me. I'm an altar boy!"

Jennifer rolled her eyes laughing.

John closed his locker and turned to look at her. "Tell me what you know."

"Apparently someone tried to break in the front door by picking the lock. A neighbor got suspicious, and as soon as the door was opened an alarm went off. The neighbor yelled at the would-be burglar to stop. The intruder just ran away."

John looked pensive. "So Dana's house now has an alarm system. What was the description of the trespasser?"

"He was a short, overweight man," replied Jennifer.

"Why did they question you?"

"Dana's dad was furious with the police and insisted that I had something to do with it."

"Whoever tried to break in didn't get the opportunity to steal what they were looking for. What day of the week does Dana's dad run his cattle auction?" asked John.

"Today. He would get home really late on auction night, which meant that every Tuesday evening Dana would hang out with me." Jennifer looked at her watch and said, "Gotta run to the courthouse."

"No!" John replied firmly. "I need a minute to pray." John just closed his eyes and began to pray.

Jennifer watched him, amazed that he prayed so much. Whenever she closed her eyes to pray, she just got a feeling like she was talking to nobody. God seemed so distant to her in prayer, which is why she was curious about John's natural tendency.

After a minute passed, John opened his eyes and looked at Jennifer. "I need the combo to Dana's house."

"Not without me, we'll go tonight together."

"No!" John said with a tone of authority.

Jennifer saw from his eyes that he wanted her to concede to him. To concede went contrary to her nature. *Maybe the problem is my nature and not his.* Regardless of the reasoning, John wanted Jennifer to trust his decision. She came to the conclusion that this matter was more important to him than her, so she submissively replied to his request by saying, "7215."

"Thank you. When is your meeting with the DA?"

"Four, but go at night, it will be safer," she replied.

John ignored her suggestion and continued, "Did Dana have a laptop or desktop?"

"Laptop."

"Digital camera?"

"No, iPhone."

"Do you know her passwords?"

"Yes."

John pointed out Jennifer's mom entering the school building. "I'll call you later."

Chapter 19

After Jennifer left with her mom, John drove to a neighborhood that backed up to Dana's. He waited patiently viewing the house from the backyard. He looked down at his watch again and noticed it was now 4 p.m. He scanned the area in all directions and saw no one watching him. Although his gut feeling was that this break-in would not go as smoothly as the first one, he felt compelled to continue. He knelt down to tighten his tennis shoe laces. His sweatshirt hood was positioned over his head with the strings pulled tightly, hiding most of his face.

As he walked through Dana's backyard, he kept repeating the Bible verse, "I shall walk through the valley of death and fear no evil."

As he approached the house from the rear, the first thing he noticed was that the garage was vacant and no cars were in the driveway. His hands were shaking so badly that it was difficult for him to put on his gloves. He tried to press 7215 into the digital lock but kept pushing the wrong numbers. On his fourth attempt, he was successful. He opened the door and quickly walked toward Dana's bedroom.

Terror and fright filled his mind like never before. He tried to pray but found it difficult. Never in his life had he experienced such feelings of isolation and fear. He repeated once again, "I shall walk through the valley of death and fear no evil" but found little comfort in the words.

As he opened Dana's bedroom door, he once again had the feeling that he wasn't alone. The burglar alarm went off with a blaring siren. Although he was expecting the deafening sound, the reality of the situation sent chills down his spine. The alarm made it known that the police were on their way and neighbors could be arriving outside any minute.

From the doorway, he saw her laptop and iPhone on the far side of the bedroom on the desk. He decided to run for them, but just as he took his second step, the bottom dresser door opened, which sent him tumbling over. His head hit the side of the dresser so hard that it dazed him. He found himself lying on the bedroom floor confused. His mind was filled with thoughts telling him not to get up. The noise of the burglar alarm siren blaring began to overwhelm him with fear. A sense of despair overtook him.

With all the strength he could muster, he mumbled, "St. Michael, help me!" He returned to his feet, stumbled to Dana's desk, and picked up her laptop and iPhone.

He looked down at the dresser drawer that tripped him up. He told himself, "Just fear offending Jesus and never fear evil." Taking a breath seemed to use most of his energy, and he felt physically exhausted. His thoughts of confusion intensified. A warm liquid ran down his face. He assessed the warm fluid with his free hand and noticed it was blood. His eyes drifted to the floor and noticed his blood mingled where Dana's was.

He wondered where his sense of clarity had gone. Horror filled his thoughts. He wished the siren would stop blaring. Despair once again tried to take him over. The thought occurred to him that he was experiencing what damned souls would experience for eternity. "Lord, help me save souls from such a horrible fate," he prayed.

John's legs felt so heavy that it was difficult for him to take a step. Breathing was strenuous. However, he forced one foot in front of the other until he reached the bedroom door. He noticed that the burglar alarm siren turned off … or was turned off. He didn't know how, but he was glad it was off.

Once he reached the threshold of Dana's bedroom door, he leaned against the wall and briefly rested. He could now hear faint police sirens getting louder. *The police will be turning into her neighborhood any moment.* He looked down at the iPhone and computer, which he could be killed for.

Chapter 20

It was Wednesday, just days before the town's annual harvest parade. "In order to decorate the float in just the next couple of nights, we need everything in place. Who has the packing tape, glue, and scissors?" Jack, the fall float coordinator, looked up from his clipboard.

Jill's eyes left the auditorium door and returned her focus on Jack. "I have them in my knapsack."

"Great. I'll mark those items off my list." Jack turned his attention to the small crowd of volunteers and continued to review his checklist.

Jill pretended to listen, but her thoughts were elsewhere. Moments earlier she noticed Jennifer slip into the school auditorium, which used to be their frequent meeting place last year. Jill took a deep breath. *I wonder if she's sneaking a drink? Lord, her cross is too heavy to carry alone, help her!* Just then it occurred to her that maybe she witnessed Jennifer sneaking into the auditorium because it was God's will for her to help. *John always says there are no coincidences with God.*

A prompting nudged Jill to find Jennifer. Moments later, she found herself scaling the stairs of the empty and barely lit auditorium. She looked up at the last tier of steps, knowing that around the corner was their old place.

Jill found Jennifer sitting alone by a large series of windows, which offered some natural light to the auditorium. "Want some company?"

Jennifer's eyes met Jill's and returned to gaze out the window overlooking the school parking lot. "Have you talked with John today?"

Jill took Jennifer's question as an opportunity to sit down and join her. "No, I talked a little with him last night. I needed to go over a couple of things with him regarding the club's code of conduct, but he pushed it off to another time. It was obvious he didn't want to talk, so my call was brief."

"I received a two-word text from him last night, but that was it."

"What's going on? Is John in danger?"

"This must be kept a secret. I think we're both in danger. He broke into Dana's yesterday afternoon."

"What's going on? I heard that some guy tried to break into her house on Sunday night."

"Someone did try on Sunday night but was chased away. It gets better because someone broke into my house yesterday afternoon and ransacked my room. Needless to say, I didn't sleep very well." Jennifer turned and gave Jill a teasing smile. "I almost called you up to invite you over again."

Jill returned the smile. "You should have. What's all this about?"

"Dana kept some incriminating evidence on a couple of people, and it seems as though these people want it. The good news is that John's text last night said he got it."

Jill stiffened. "Is that why that guy followed John to my party on Saturday night?"

"He wasn't following John but me. We now refer to him as my 'secret admirer.' Monday, he followed me out of school to the park. He must suspect that I'm on to him because he's kept his distance ever since."

"You guys need to go to the police."

"It's complicated. I wish we could. The good news is that John thinks this will all be over in a couple of days."

"Can I do anything to help?"

Jennifer nodded her head 'no' and then got really excited. "Look at the car driving past the guard house. Is that John?"

Jill looked into the school parking lot and replied no, then continued, "You really like him."

Jennifer's eyes left the parking lot, and she looked at Jill. "It shows?"

"A lot."

"I've never clicked with a guy so well. He treats me like a person who should be loved and cherished, which is a fresh change of pace from the other guys I've dated."

"Has John expressed those feelings toward you?"

"You know John; he's guarded. I think he genuinely likes my company." Jennifer noticed Jill taking a deep breath. "I know what you're thinking. A lot of girls more his type have expressed an interest in him only to be disappointed."

"Jennifer, you're a wonderful person, but John has a clear vision of what he's looking for in a girl."

"I know he's in a different world than I am."

Thank you Lord for the perfect opportunity to evangelize her. "Jen, would you like to enter his world? All you have to do is ask Jesus to forgive you. I can help you. Let's do it right now."

Jennifer kindly smiled at Jill. "Thank you, but John and I had this conversation. It's a little more complicated than that."

Jill looked puzzled. "How so?"

"John told me that when I ask God for His forgiveness then I have to begin forgiving others. That means I have to forgive Dana, who convinced me to have an abortion; and I have to forgive Peter, who talked me into the abortion and who continues to be cruel to me. Did you know that he's supplying the police with motives for why I had a reason to kill Dana?"

Compassion filled Jill's face. *Unless you forgive others, you cannot be forgiven.* "Peter and Dana will be held accountable before God one day, but you will be, too. No one made you abort your child; ultimately, you chose to do it. John is right, you must forgive them or else your unforgiveness will be like a cancer that slowly eats you away." Jill waited for Jennifer to look at her and then continued, "Do you know who you have to forgive the most?"

"Who?"

"Yourself. Deep down you're beating yourself up over your past. You need to give it to God and become a new person. You'll find happiness if you do." Jill began playing with her pen.

Jennifer tried to plead her innocence. *Denial temporarily soothes the conscience better than truth to the unrepentant soul.* "But the abortion wasn't my fault. I was talked into it by Peter, who wanted to save his future political career, and by Dana, who wanted drug money."

"In some ways your decision was no different than anyone else's who has an abortion. Sixty percent of women walking in for an abortion were on contraceptives. In addition, most women who have an abortion find little support from friends or family. Most of them feel coerced."

Jennifer protested, "But mine was different. I was surrounded by evil. I was talked into it because of some self-serving reasons of those people closest to me, even my own mom, who had to give parental consent. She said she didn't want to raise the baby or see me throw away my plans to become a nurse!"

"Every abortion is an evil plot." Jill could tell that she was losing Jennifer on this point, so she decided to explain her thoughts in more detail. "Have you ever had bad thoughts in a situation, which were in conflict with thoughts that you knew to be good and true?"

"Of course, that voice was screaming at me not to go through with the abortion, while at the same time I had Peter and Dana telling me 'just to do it and get on with your life.' "

"The devil can only tempt us by placing bad thoughts in our mind. It's his normal mode of operation in leading souls away from God. He does this to everyone to some degree, just some more than others. Although you heard the evil words spoken through Dana and Peter; nevertheless, you chose to do an act that deep down you knew was wrong."

Jennifer really didn't want to continue this conversation. "I do regret my abortion."

"Regretting it is good but not enough. You need contrition. It will require that you change in such a way that if the decision had to be made over again, this 'new Jennifer' would not have done it in the first place. What I'm trying to say is you need a change of heart."

"All this murder stuff will be over this week, and then I'll have a chance to think about what you and John are telling me. My plan is to ask John to take me to church again once this is all behind me. Then I'll ask him to help me work through my unforgiveness and ask God to forgive me."

"What if you die tonight?"

"Then I guess I'll go where I deserve."

Jill closed her eyes and tried to collect her thoughts on how to best reply.

Jennifer took the pause as an opportunity to address a question that has been nagging her. "Can we change the subject?"

Jill reluctantly nodded yes.

"Can I confide in you? Why do I have these strong feelings

about Peter that won't go away. About an hour ago, he purposely kissed some girl in front of me. To top it off, he stared at me the whole time he kissed her. If any other guy at school did that to me, I wouldn't have cared less, but the things he does really bother me. I can't figure my feelings out because a month ago, I wanted to break up with him. I have no interest in ever getting back together with him. None of my old boyfriends have ever had that effect on me."

Jill sighed. Then the answer came to her, and she smiled internally at God's providence. She pulled out a roll of packing tape and superglue. She ripped off a foot-long piece of tape and asked Jennifer to hold out her arm. Then she stuck the tape across Jennifer's forearm.

The sight of packing tape across her arm scared Jennifer. "How are you going to remove that tape without hurting me?"

Jill smiled and ignored her question. "God designed the bond created between a husband and wife not to be broken. It's more than physical; it's emotional and spiritual. When an unmarried couple tries to enjoy these gifts meant for marriage, the bond is still created. I suspect your relationship with Peter was different than the others in this way."

Jill quickly ripped off the tape.

Jennifer winced in pain, "Ow! That hurt! Look at all the hair you pulled off!"

"Good! God designed it to be painful because the bond is not supposed to be separated." Jill put the same piece of tape back on Jennifer's arm and pulled it off again. "How did that feel?"

"Not as bad."

Jill repeated the gesture six times until the tape wouldn't adhere anymore. Jennifer stated that she didn't feel any more pain.

"If you continue to sinfully enjoy the marital gifts outside marriage, the physical, emotional, and spiritual bonds would be lessened with each relationship. Years later, when you decide to marry, the glue that God intended to help a marriage to stay together would be almost nonexistent. The physical, emotional, and spiritual bond God designed the couple to have would be gone. Is this what you want for your marriage?"

With all sincerity, Jennifer replied no.

Jill began to cover the tape with superglue. "The good news is that God allows the bond to be restored. The ordinary tape represents human love, which is all that most married couples experience. Human love is good, but by grace we can share in God's uncreated divine love. When two Christians marry and truly share His love in their souls, it's like a superglue bond they enjoy."

Jennifer expressed horror at the sight of Jill layering the packing tape with superglue. "You're not planning on putting that tape coated in superglue on my arm?"

Jill smiled. "Tell me, which bond do you want for holding together your marriage?"

"I definitely want my bond to be made with the superglue bond because I know that it would be strong. Marriages today need a strong bond to stand the tests of life that try to pull them apart. Also, because the bond is stronger, it would seem as though the marriage would be happier." Looking down at the superglue, she ended with, "But I shudder at the thought if such a bond was ever broken."

"Right. Your insight is right on. The analogy applies to your pain with Peter."

"What you're saying makes sense. I know it's true. My past

is full of regrets." Jennifer got agitated as she watched a Ford Explorer drive by. "Look! There goes my secret admirer."

Jill turned and looked out the window. "Doesn't it make you a little nervous?"

"I'm terrified."

Chapter 21

As soon as the campaign headquarters' phone was picked up, Jim inquired, "Is The Witch in?"

Belinda smiled, "Your boss occasionally answers the phone, so one of these days you're going to be sorry."

"Have I ever told you that I'm invincible?"

"Only about a hundred times." Belinda started to play with her hair. "I don't know if you're invincible, but you have been invisible. So what rock have you been hiding under the last couple of days?"

"Only snakes hide under rocks. Would you like to rephrase that question?"

Belinda playfully answered, "No, but have I ever told you that I like snakes?"

"What are your favorite snakes?"

Belinda's eyes lit up. "Powerful ones!"

"You need to lie and wait for a little while because invincibility is about to evolve into raw power."

"I'll wait impatiently." Belinda noticed Eleanor's line just went dead. "She just hung up. Let me transfer you. Bye."

As soon as Jim heard Eleanor join the line, he turned on his recorder. "Eleanor, it's Jim."

"I hope you're enjoying your stay in Governor Wilson's quaint hometown. Thanks for checking in. Are you on your way back with Dana's laptop and iPhone?"

"We had a setback."

Eleanor's friendly tone changed. "What do you mean *we* had a setback? *You* had a setback."

"I negotiated with Dana's dad to buy her estate, which was to include her laptop and iPhone. I went over there late yesterday afternoon to pick it up just to find out his house had been burglarized an hour before I arrived."

"Don't tell me Dana's laptop and iPhone were stolen."

"You're a mind reader."

She became furious. "This isn't good."

Jim decided to let her fret and hold back the good news. "You know who's been hanging around Berryville?"

Eleanor dryly replied, "I give up."

"Gene Simpson, and he hasn't been hanging around the campaign office, either."

"That is strange. With six days to the election, I would have guessed he'd be busy at the headquarters in the capitol."

"I think he's looking for the same things we are."

"He must have found out that Dana had a damning picture of Peter." In a demanding tone Eleanor continued, "I WANT that picture. Maybe Gene broke in yesterday, and he has the computer."

"No, Gene tried to break in on Sunday night, but a neighbor chased him away. I was following him yesterday afternoon. He broke into Jennifer's house while Dana's room was being broken into." Jim laughed, "So he has an alibi."

Eleanor didn't laugh. Humor never really interested her. "Certainly, you called the police."

Jim used a serious tone. "I was in no condition to call the police."

"Why?" Eleanor demanded.

"I was laughing too hard. He used a stepladder to enter her bedroom window. When he got about half way in the window, the ladder fell over. He got stuck, and all I could see were his short, stubby legs floundering in the air. It was quite a site. I felt so sorry for him that I almost went over and gave him a push."

"I never knew you had an altruistic side."

Jim laughed quietly at the thought. "I believe John Lightman has Dana's electronics."

"How do you know that?"

"Dana's dad had a security camera installed in the house. He was viewing the footage of the robbery when I showed up to buy Dana's estate. Although the robber wore a hood, it sure looked like John Lightman's build. I recognized him because he's been hanging out with Peter's ex-girlfriend, Jennifer. I think they have a fling going on. It gets more interesting, though. Today, I was poking around John's house and saw a stack of the governor's re-election yard signs leaning against the house. I asked some questions at the local campaign office. It turns out that John's mom has been a longtime volunteer for Governor Wilson!"

Eleanor became elated. "This is great. Do you have any evidence of the fling?"

"I have a picture of them in the park just about to kiss."

Eleanor started bubbling. "You're wonderful. Send the picture to me ASAP. Do you think that this John kid took the evidence to the police?"

"No. I thought that exact thing, so I hung around the police station all morning waiting for him to show up, but he never did. I had a long talk with the detective assigned to the case, and there's no change; Jennifer is going to be indicted any day. The head detective told me the investigation was over. He's received no new information."

"Maybe you need to go to John's house tonight and retrieve Dana's laptop and iPhone."

"Your wish is my command." Jim felt a sense of nausea overtake him with such an expression of humility.

"Anything else?"

"I bugged Jennifer's house as you requested. I heard Jennifer telling a girlfriend that Peter started dating Dana a couple of days before the murder."

"A love triangle! I love this. You're making my day! What else?"

"I also heard her tell her friend that last week she almost committed suicide by taking a bottle of sleeping pills. This John guy talked her out of it at the last minute."

Too bad. "Anything else?"

"Sunday morning, John told her that Dana was paid to talk her into an abortion."

A brief moment of terror came over Eleanor. She played ignorant, "I knew Dana was collecting information about Peter and his family. What is this 'she was being paid to talk her into an abortion'?"

Jim could tell she knew more than she was revealing. "Apparently, Dana was paid a bonus if she could persuade Jennifer to have Peter pay for her abortion. Her intention was to create a scandal for our pro-family governor."

Eleanor became serious. "What else?"

"That was about it. I almost forgot, but Jennifer mentioned that she played tennis with the governor on numerous occasions, too."

"That tidbit of information will be useful. Anything more?"

"Just that Jennifer took the news about being set up for an abortion pretty hard.

"Is she suicidal again?"

"I suspect she's on the edge."

"Is she a Christian?"

"No."

Good! Tomorrow, I'll give her a nudge. "I'll drop a letter in the mail to Dana's grandmother, who's been a long-time liberal activist. Tomorrow morning, her Grandma will be returning from a month-long vacation. Soon, in her mail will be a letter from Dana sharing with her the details of the governor's scandal and the paperwork from the abortion provider. Since Dana took Jennifer for the abortion, she was in a position to have kept the paperwork. She made sure that Peter's name was on the paperwork as the father. Anyway, the letter is asking her for advice on how to handle the secret scandal. The letter also mentions that Dana fears for her life if the governor found out what she knew."

"Brilliant. What about the post mark date?"

"I have connections everywhere. I had it stamped a day before her murder from the Berryville post office."

"What will Dana's grandma do with this info?"

"She'll head to the nearest TV station. I'm sure of that."

Jim became concerned. "A public scandal might shove Jennifer over the edge."

A sense of perverse joy filled Eleanor's heart. *I hope so.* "She probably knows too much anyway. A public scandal regarding her abortion might make her not sleep well. Maybe you could see to it she receives a full bottle of sleeping pills once the scandal breaks."

You are evil. Jim joked, "Now you're showing your altruistic side."

Jim turned off his phone's recorder as he hung up.

Chapter 22

Jennifer was stressed out about John's whereabouts all day at school. Her last communication with him was a text last night, simply "Got it."

The familiar sound of the last school bell echoed through the hall. Jennifer rushed to John's locker but ended up standing alone as students brushed by. She wiped a tear away. Although they didn't share any classes, normally she could find him. *Did he get into trouble breaking into Dana's? Maybe he bumped into Dana's killer? Is he hurt?* No matter how hard she tried to dispel endless negative thoughts, she couldn't get them out of her mind.

Knowing that her mom was waiting outside to drive her home, she headed for the parking lot.

Jennifer greeted her mom and got in the car. Just as they were about to pull away, John appeared at the driver's side window and motioned to Jennifer's mom to roll the window down.

While he waited for her window to open, John glanced over at Jennifer. He noticed that her face lit up and she flashed a wide smile.

"Hi, Mrs. Lawson. I was wondering if Jennifer could join me for a prayer session this afternoon. There'll be pizza afterward."

Mrs. Lawson considered the proposal. She desperately wanted Jennifer to hang around a different crowd from school. *Maybe we'd get along better if she hung out with polite students like John.* She liked the positive influence that Christians brought to the community but personally didn't want anything to do with religion.

Looking at John with trust, Jennifer's mom answered, "Since I'm sure you will keep her out of trouble, it's okay with me."

Jennifer responded to her mom's comment by rolling her eyes and throwing her head back. John struggled to keep a straight face given Jennifer's melodramatic response.

Turning to her daughter, she asked, "Jen, do you want to go with him?"

In a serious tone that almost expressed contrition, Jennifer replied, "I think I need to."

◆ ◆ ◆

Jennifer was so relieved to know John was okay that she almost burst into tears of joy walking to his car. Once at his car, she put her hair in a ponytail as they drove away.

With an old English accent, Jennifer began the verbal folly she enjoyed with John, "My tears almost supplemented the evening dew, my lord. Thy absence weighed heavily on thy maid's heart."

John joined in, "Did thou not knowest I couldst be found in Our Father's house?"

Jennifer looked at him with a surprised look, "What is mine is thine, so why did thou entereth thy maid's father's household like a thief in the night?"

John corrected her misunderstanding. "I entered not liketh a thief in thy family's house. Rather, I entered as a poor unworthy servant into Our Father's house. Our Father's house is a house of prayer."

"My lord, forgive my mistake for thou and I liveth in different worlds; we speaketh different languages."

"My fair maid, to error is human. Thou needest to soar with the eagles and embrace the divine."

Jennifer asked for his patience. "Thy maid, I feareth, is a

mere eaglet and cannot yet flyeth. Thus patience must be embraced by my king."

A look of concern crossed John's face as he understood someone broke into her house. "O most fair maid, thy king will waiteth till the sun stops shining for thou to taketh flight. Pray telleth, thy father's house had a thief in the night?"

"Yea, my lord, but not in the night. The crime happened at the appointed hour of my inquisition with the magistrate."

"It was not I, my lady, thy king haveth an alibi. See, I was a thief in another house. I have a computer and phone, which proveth my innocence."

Jennifer laughed as she asked, "A stolen computer and phone proves thy innocence? Hast thou gone mad, my lord, with such a defense? But still, my heart deligheth that ye are only guilty of one crime and not two! Did thou goeth to Our Father's house all day to repent of such a crime?"

John put on a comical grin and continued, "No my lady, I repented not but pray, yes. But what placeth such a thought on thy lips? Maybe, doeth thou dreameth of going to Our Father's house to repent?"

Jennifer smiled back and innocently teased him, "If I knew thou resided in Our Father's house, I wouldst gladly repenteth a thousand times to be by thy side."

John found her witty comeback amusing. "Our Father shared good news for my maid. The chain is to be unlocked, the prison door opened, and my maid set free forever!"

"When, my lord?"

"Before the moon traveleth the evening sky tonight, thou will be free from the terrible weight that hath crushed thy soul."

Chapter 23

Jennifer shouted with excitement and dropped the accent. "Let me get this correct. You went to church today and prayed. God told you that tonight I would be set free? What exactly did He say?"

"I heard the sentence enter my heart, 'Tonight you will set Jennifer free.' I could be wrong so don't get your hopes up too high."

"You're never wrong. Of course, today is day nine of your novena. By ten you'll set me free. I wish I knew a way to show you how grateful I am."

"A simple thank you would suffice."

"Obviously, you don't know anything about these things so I don't know why I even discuss them with you," Jennifer replied in jest.

John didn't reply as he turned his car down a farm road. He traveled just a short distance before he turned the car off.

"Why are we here?"

"We're going to spend a couple of hours overlooking that bluff. This farm belongs to a friend of my father's. If he sees my car parked here, he won't think anything of it. Help me carry some items."

John handed her a sleeping bag as he grabbed a telescope and some binoculars. The two positioned themselves on a bluff overlooking a valley below. Several buildings were surrounded by hundreds of acres of rolling pasture land.

In a theatrical tone, Jennifer teased, "Sitting on a bluff watching the sunset, followed by gazing at the stars with a telescope, how romantic."

John replied playfully, "Maybe from your world, but I see darkness approaching. The stars are nothing but eyes from heaven watching our every thought, word, and deed. The bluff is nothing more than a reminder of the deep abyss that awaits us if we fail the test on earth." He changed his voice to invoke a scary tone, "and just inches under where we sit are lurking thousands of earthworms waiting to consume our dead bodies."

With a slight squint, Jennifer replied, "I think I like my world better than yours. What's so wrong with romance and love?"

"I believe romance and love can be good." John needed to change the subject. "I need to give you a mission. Use these binoculars and watch the activity of those two buildings below. This is part of Mr. Keller's sale barn. A truck is expected from Mexico soon, and I want to see what happens."

"Eye-eye captain," she replied as she accepted her assignment.

"While you do that, I'm going to view her laptop. What is Dana's password?"

"Dana1999. So how did your burglary go yesterday?"

"Not good."

"What happened?"

"Remember when we broke in last week, and I told you that I had the feeling that we weren't alone? Well, we weren't. Her room is heavily infested with demons. This might be hard for you to believe, but it's true. I've never been so attacked in my life!"

"How were you attacked?"

"I had horrible feelings of despair and hopelessness. When I tried to run through the room, I saw the bottom drawer open and trip me up. I almost passed out. Part of me had the feeling that I'd never escape her room."

Jennifer put down the binoculars and looked at him, "You're scaring me. Is that how you got the cut on your head?"

"Yeah. I struggled with all my might to exit her room. Once out of the room, everything went back to normal."

"Is that why you skipped school?"

"Yes. After being attacked by an onslaught of demons, I felt that I needed to regroup spiritually."

"Why do you think you didn't feel the demons as strongly last week when we broke in?"

John replied matter-of-factly, "Maybe God wanted to show me that I need you by my side as I fight the demons in this life."

Jennifer just smiled at the thought. Since John never indicated that he needed her, she assumed he was joking. "A couple of minutes ago, you said you believed in romance and love. How does your idea of love differ from mine?"

"You love that your world gives you things pleasing to your senses. The pleasures of this world come to you in many ways. For example, it might be enjoying a romantic moment while on a casual date."

"So what's wrong with that?"

John looked at her thoughtfully, "Nothing, as long it's ordered correctly. Most people live for nothing other than an endless variety of pleasures that are pleasing to the senses. These unceasing cravings for pleasures leave the soul unsatisfied and empty and leave people always wanting more. It is not that all pleasures are bad, but living for them, especially the illegitimate ones, make them become so evil."

"So a romantic moment can be good in your world?" Jennifer asked with a slight tease.

"Yes, but friends don't share them." John cleared his throat to make his point known. "I personally believe that all romantic moments should be shared within marriage. How would you like every ex-boyfriend and fling to show up at your wedding?"

Jennifer was silent. John noticed she was slightly uncomfortable with the thought.

John continued, "I'd like to live my life in such a way that I could welcome every ex-girlfriend to my wedding. In addition, I'd like to live my life in such a way that my wedding video could have pictures from any part of my dating history and not provoke an ounce of shame or regret." John turned and looked at Jennifer. With a serious tone, he continued, "Deep down can you see a great good in my way of life?"

Jennifer sincerely replied, "Yes, even though I see how noble your ideas are, I'm not sure I want to give up my way of life. I guess I'm addicted to earthly candy, but I'm beginning to value truly good things as well, like our friendship."

"I can tell you appreciate our friendship and will make sacrifices for me." He ended with a teasing jab, "So you're not all bad."

"Thank you … I think! I've wondered if you noticed the things I've done."

Wanting to show his gratitude, John decided to name the little sacrifices he had seen her do. "I notice more than you think. For example, yesterday's hug at my locker was far less assertive than a normal, full-contact hug."

"I thought you'd appreciate that type of hug better. I sensed you felt uncomfortable with my hug last Friday."

John replied looking at her, "You assumed correctly. I can tell that your attire all week has been modest and not that trendy, tight, revealing stuff that's in style, which you know I hate."

"You don't miss anything. I told you that I want to be a true friend to you, and if these little things help our friendship out, I'm glad to do them."

"Also, I noticed how you distanced me from yourself when Detective Scott asked about us. By doing that, you protected me, whereas saying otherwise may have benefitted you." John turned on Dana's iPhone and entered the four-digit code Jennifer gave him to see texts, photos, e-mails, etc. "How does it make you feel making little sacrifices for something genuinely good?"

In a tone of authenticity, Jennifer replied, "I feel good inside."

"You can see the value in a true love, like our friendship, and it makes you feel good inside. Good news, you're not completely lost, just a little fallen."

Jennifer pretended not to hear him.

John decided to change the subject, "So, how did your plea bargain go with the DA yesterday?"

"Since I wouldn't confess to the crime, it didn't go well."

"So during your meeting with the DA, someone broke into your house?"

"Yes, they went through my room, my mom's room, and the living room."

"Let me guess, your room was ransacked the most. Your laptop and phone were taken."

Jennifer wondered how he guessed that. "How'd you know?"

"I bet the same person who tried to break into Dana's the previous night broke into yours. He was looking for Dana's things. I suspect they want the file that I'm looking at as we speak. Dana's laptop has a couple of interesting items on it. Since you were best friends with Dana, they guessed you might also have this file. Because 'the short, overweight guy' almost got caught breaking into Dana's the previous night, he thought your home would be an easier target than going back to hers."

Jennifer decided to give him an update on the scene below. "I see Dana's dad walking around doing some chores. There is a Mexican man who just pulled up and started talking with him. He looks familiar, but I can't place him." In a huge burst of excitement Jennifer exclaimed, "That's Officer Manuel standing beside Dana's dad! He isn't in uniform, but it looks like him. That jerk was at Dana's murder scene and says I confessed to the murder, but I don't remember anything of the sort."

"Let me see!"

Jennifer handed him the binoculars and asked, "So, what's so interesting on Dana's computer?"

"The files of everyone she was trying to blackmail. Some pictures, notes, and audio recordings." John changed the subject as he continued to look through the binoculars, "A large stock trailer just showed up and is backing up to the corral. Officer Manuel is gone. He must have gone inside."

"What's the fastest way one can enter your world?"

"Trusting your conversion to the Mother of God is probably the fastest way." John turned off Dana's computer and added, "Let's pray a rosary now. It might be better if I keep the binoculars while we pray."

Jennifer smirked at the thought, "You're going to pray as you look through binoculars?"

"Yes, I am. Although setting aside time every day for focused, reverent prayer is essential, the rest of the day should be filled with prayer whenever possible. Anytime one is not sinning, one can pray." John began the rosary out loud, and Jennifer tried to follow along with her eyes closed. Twenty minutes later, they were finished. Jennifer felt refreshed but still had a lot of questions.

John called into town for a carry-out pizza and asked Jennifer to pick it up while he watched the stock trailer drive to the corner of the lot, where the drivers began cleaning it out.

Unknown to Jennifer, during her errand she would bump into the man who broke into her bedroom yesterday.

Chapter 24

Gene Simpson's round stature felt sandwiched in the booth at the pizza parlor, whereas, Peter, a moderately proportioned teenager, felt far more comfortable. It had been several days since their last meeting, and there was a lot to catch up on.

Gene shoved the fourth slice of pizza into his mouth. "It appears that someone got Dana's laptop before I did. Do you know who might have wanted it?"

Peter preferred staring at his pizza rather than his dinner mate. "Jennifer."

"Why would Jennifer want it?"

"Probably to clear her name of the crime or hide something that might be used against her."

Gene challenged Peter's assumption. "She was at the police station when Dana's laptop was stolen. Interestingly enough, someone broke into her room at the same time that Dana's room was burglarized." Gene pretended to be innocent, but this gesture didn't fool Peter.

A feeling of anger rose in Peter. "Then her new boyfriend did it for her."

Gene grabbed another slice of pizza. "Sounds like you miss her."

"I wish I never met her."

Gene repeated himself, but his joke fell on deaf ears. Peter pretended not to hear him.

"Tell me what you know about her new boyfriend."

Peter answered dryly. "John Lightman. A senior. His mom has been a long-term volunteer for Dad."

"Could his mom be a plant?"

Peter took a sip of water. "I don't think so."

You're so naïve! What do you know about these things? "We'll see."

Peter became inquisitive. "I have a political question for you. Polls show Americans are becoming increasingly pro-life. You think abortion will ever be outlawed?"

Why an interest in abortion? Gene finally wiped some cheese that has been hanging from his chin. "Not in your lifetime."

Peter was disappointed in the answer. "Why?"

"Keep this to yourself." Gene straightened up and leaned toward Peter so as not to be overheard. "You know most elections are only decided by a percentage or two. Twenty-one percent of Republican votes are single-issue, anti-abortion voters. If they didn't have this issue, our studies have shown 1/3 of these single-issue voters would embrace the socialism Democrats offer. This would spell disaster to the Republican party."

"I find that hard to believe."

"It's true. The Republicans want a close fight with abortion, but they have no interest in winning. Abortion would have been outlawed years ago if this wasn't the case." Gene could tell Peter needed some facts. "Look at the list of pro-abortion Supreme Court appointments by pro-life Republican presidents—Sandra Day O'Connor, David Souter, Anthony Kennedy, John Paul Stevens! If just one of those appointments were not pro-abortion, then Roe v. Wade could have been overturned years ago."

"Bastards!"

Gene belched a laugh. "Yes, they are. There have been numerous challenges to Roe v. Wade over the past forty years, and all the battles were lost by just one vote." Gene became reflective. "Knowing that we have to sacrifice a huge part of the next generation is probably the ugliest part of the election business."

Peter looked at him in disbelief.

"If you don't believe me, consider this. In contrast, how many pro-life Supreme Court appointments have the Democrats accidently put in place over the past forty years? Zero."

The conversation seemed to paralyze Peter.

Gene took advantage of the situation and grabbed the last slice of pizza.

"If what you're saying is true, then why don't the Democrats let Roe verses Wade be overturned instead of fighting the issue tooth and nail?"

Gene was impressed with Peter's insight. "Last election, I worked for the other side and asked some of the higher ups that exact question. My job is to win at all costs, and I'm convinced that the Democrats could create a landslide with such a strategy. It was one of those political conversations the higher-ups would never want public. I found out the answer to your question. The answer I received was that abortion was more of a religion to them. It seems as though they want abortions more than winning." Gene struggled to hold in another belch. "Peter, you're displaying stronger pro-life convictions than your father."

Peter was upset but only mildly displayed his emotions. Although he lobbied Jennifer for the abortion, his conscience tortured him ever since. He saw abortion as the only way to save his family from scandal, but the price he paid was high. Guilt is a heavy load on the soul, and the web of evil around the situation only exasperated the situation. He had no interest in sharing his personal convictions with one of the vilest persons he ever met. "So all the campaign promises are lies?"

"Actually, not completely. The Republicans will gladly fight for endless restrictions, but they want it legal to rally their biggest base. The strategy is working great, and I don't see a change coming anytime soon."

Peter noticed that Jennifer just walked into the pizza parlor.

Chapter 25

Jennifer returned to the cliff with dinner. Without much enthusiasm, she said, "Eat the pizza while it's hot. What did I miss?"

As John took the pizza, he noticed Jennifer's happy disposition was gone. He bit into a slice of pizza and replied, "It appears that the stock trailer was just locked in the big shed for the night. You missed the two drivers shoveling a huge amount of manure out of the trailer. Then they power-washed the trailer clean. With the water splattering everywhere, it's safe to assume they're covered head to foot in manure."

"I think I lost my appetite," Jennifer replied matter-of-factly.

"Great, because I'm starving," John replied grinning. "Did something happen when you picked up the pizza? You look upset."

"Peter was sitting in a booth with Gene Simpson, his dad's campaign manager. It was humiliating because they kept looking at me. It was obvious they were talking about me. At one point Gene stared at me for a long time. He gave me the creeps."

"Don't tell me, Gene is short and overweight."

"How did you know?"

"I bet the tall shelves in your bedroom were not burglarized."

"Yes, you're right. Those shelves were untouched." Jennifer became concerned. "It freaks me out knowing that I just bumped into the man who burglarized my bedroom. He definitely fits the description of the burglar who tried to break into Dana's the previous night."

"We need to be more careful in the future. I believe we both might be in danger."

"I suspect Peter and Gene would want the file in Dana's laptop."

John replied, "Bingo! That would be my guess. Did they follow you out?"

"No, I looked back numerous times because the whole situation worried me." A malicious look came across Jennifer's face. "Peter is making my life so miserable. I would love Dana's picture to rub his nose in it a little."

"I know Peter is feeding my uncle very damaging information regarding you, but you must forgive him and wish him well. If you don't, over time it will make you miserable."

Jennifer, expressing a little irritation regarding her duty to forgive, blurted, "You already told me that I needed to forgive. I'll think about it, but no promises." Jennifer didn't want to continue discussing this topic, so she asked, "What did you find out tonight during our stakeout? I haven't noticed anything unusual."

"You haven't noticed anything unusual because you're a city girl, and I'm a country boy. Think about what just happened. Two Mexican drivers just dropped off a load of cattle, which originated 3000 miles away from here, and probably didn't pay their gas bill. Although they'd been driving the stock trailer for two days straight, they took the time to clean out the trailer before going home. Since the next load of horses won't go out for three days, why the rush to clean the trailer? Why not just go home, get some rest, and come back and clean the trailer tomorrow? In addition, why lock a stinky stock trailer in the shed? Finally, that shed has security cameras all around it, for what purpose, to guard a worthless stock trailer? To tell you the truth, this whole operation smells."

"You suspect they're smuggling drugs? But why send a load of horses to Mexico just to buy a load of cows."

"The smell of manure would overwhelm any scent smelling dogs might pick up on at the border crossings. In addition, what border agent would want to crawl around a poopy stock trailer looking for drugs?"

"That's brilliant!" Jennifer said enthusiastically.

"Are you getting your appetite back?"

"Yeah, pass me a slice."

"Let's load up. Here, take the box of pizza; you can eat all you want in the car. Dana's dad just left the sale barn lot. He was the last to leave. I'm going to drop you off at the gas station by the edge of town. I want to return and look at the empty stock trailer they have sitting at the far edge of the lot over there. It must be a backup trailer for their operation."

"I want to go with you."

"I know you want to, but I won't let you. The lot has cameras all over it, and you're already not on Mr. Keller's Christmas card list. I suspect the security system will trigger a call to the police, and I don't want you in any more trouble."

"Fine, but I want it noted for the record that I'm doing it your way under protest," Jennifer said with a sense of conviction.

"Your protest is noted. I'll let you off here. Hang out inside the gas station. If I'm not back in thirty minutes, call my uncle and tell him everything you know."

"Okay, but please be careful. I'd rather go to jail than see you hurt. Promise me you won't take any chances." A tear ran down Jennifer's cheek.

John could tell that Jennifer was choking up. "I promise."

When Jennifer watched John drive off, a sharp pain entered her stomach. The thought of something happening to John caused her emotional distress. She wiped another tear away. *A cup of coffee might calm my nerves,* she thought, heading inside the convenience store.

Minutes seemed like hours as she waited, looking out the window. The thought occurred to her that if someone killed Dana for knowing too much, John could be killed, too. Horrible regret filled her mind for asking his help. She peered helplessly out the window, eager for his return.

Two police cars, with their sirens blaring, screamed past the gas station toward the sale barn. She knew they were headed for John. She chided herself for leaving her phone in his car because she had no way to warn him.

She walked outside the gas station to look down the street. A sense of hope filled her heart when she saw John turning into the gas station.

"Jump in!" John commanded.

Jennifer noticed John repeatedly glancing in his rearview mirror. She found herself turning around to see if someone was following them as well. John seemed calm, which helped reduce her anxiety. "How did it go?"

"I got just what I needed."

"I was scared to death that something happened to you!"

"Did you try to say a prayer while I was gone or did you just fret at the gas station?"

"Honestly, the thought of praying didn't enter my mind. I'm sorry to say all I did was fret. John, please pull over here."

John complied. "Don't tell me you want a romantic walk in the park right now."

John's humor didn't defuse Jennifer's anxiety this time. "John, I couldn't live with myself if I knew that you got hurt trying to vindicate me. At the gas station, I got an incredible pain in my stomach worrying about you. I'd like us to go to the police and share everything we've found and let them figure it out. I'd rather face jail time than see you hurt."

"We don't have to go to the police department because I'm sure they'll come to us. My uncle is probably viewing the security camera tapes as we speak. He'll recognize my car right off the bat and will be waiting for me at my doorstep when I get home. I have enough information to make his day."

"Do you know who did it?"

"Not yet, but I have all the pieces of the puzzle to figure it out. I just need some time to process everything, and I think we'll have this all figured out."

A lady screaming for help broke the silence of the night. John became alarmed, "Did you just hear a scream?"

"Yes. It sounds like a girl screamed from down in the park," Jennifer said with a sense of terror.

"Call 911!" John shouted as he ran toward the sound.

Jennifer turned on her cell phone and looked out the rear of the car, where she could see John running at full speed down the hill toward the altercation. She punched in 911. "Benton Park," she answered when the dispatcher asked her location. "There's a lady screaming for help, from the south pavilion area."

As Jennifer hung up the phone, she noticed the time was 10 p.m. It occurred to her that John's nine-day novena just ended. She was about to exit the car when the thought of saying a prayer for John entered her mind. *"Dear God, help John!"* Before she could open her eyes, another thought entered her mind. It was almost if someone was talking to her heart. Since she had never heard this "voice" before, she didn't know what to make of it. Wherever it came from, the thought terrified her because this unseen voice said, "If the blood of My Son is not sufficient for you to forgive, maybe John's blood will."

Jennifer screamed at the top of her lungs "NO!"

Chapter 26

"What took you so long getting here?" Tim barked at Carlos as he entered the sale barn office.

"Nice to see you, too!" Carlos retorted sarcastically. "I do moonlight as a police officer if you forgot."

Tim stared down his partner. "We just had some kid drive up to our backup stock trailer. Look at camera #3. He opened the door and took pictures before driving away. It must be the same kid who broke into my house because the smart aleck waved again at the camera."

"Not good. You think it's the same one we caught snooping inside the shed a couple days ago?"

"I was wondering the same thing." Tim was becoming angry. "We almost had him then, but he jumped the fence and scaled the hill before we could get him."

Carlos laughed. "You hired a bunch of fat farm boys to help you with the operation. I've told you that you need some slim 'amigos' around here. If you had them, we would've caught that guy when he was sneaking around the machine shed."

Tim walked over to camera #1 and paused the video as John's car was exiting the parking lot. "Look at this shot and tell me if you can make out the plates. My eyes are getting too old to read this. I'll zoom in on the plates."

Carlos looked at a dark blur and almost laughed out loud at the thought of reading the plate. It was only the thought of Tim's angry disposition that stopped him. "I don't think I can read it. Try moving it to the right, and I'll try to read the bumper sticker."

"What does it say?"

Although Carlos couldn't read the bumper sticker, the outline was familiar enough to figure it out. "It's a Child, Not a Choice."

"I hate those people." He zoomed in on the side of the car. "Maybe we can make out the make and model."

"Blue Toyota Corolla with a dent in the right, front corner."

Tim was amazed. "Wow, you have a lot better eyesight than me if you can see all that. Now, I want you to drive around all night until you find that car. When you find out whose it is, come back and tell me. I'll do the dirty work this time."

Carlos didn't move but instead yawned.

"Now!" screamed Tim.

Carlos didn't flinch. "I know whose car it is because I see it parked often at the police station. It's John Lightman's, who happens to be Detective Peterson's nephew."

"Detective Peterson! He came by when I called 911. Don't you think he would have recognized John's car?"

Carlos nodded, "Yep."

Tim loaded his revolver, "I remember Detective Peterson was unusually quiet as he stared at the screen, but he never mentioned to me that he recognized the car."

"The fact that he drove his car right past our cameras and waved makes me feel that he didn't care about being spotted."

Tim's anger compromised his ability to reason correctly. "What does that mean?"

"It means that he must be real close to going to his uncle."

Tim returned his loaded gun to his revolver case. "I think we need to get that boy before he talks with his uncle."

"I think you're too late." Carlos said with a sly smile.

Extreme fear came across Tim's face. "Did he already talk with his uncle?"

With a devilish grin Carlos answered, "No. Someone else already got to him before we did. He just got stabbed in the park. I was there when the ambulance showed up. He's in pretty bad shape."

"Good. Did you see his car?"

Carlos pointed to the security monitor, "Yep, I noticed your friend Jennifer Lawson driving John's car to the hospital just thirty minutes ago."

Tim got excited. "Let's get his camera and Dana's stuff. Moreover, we're going to need to help those two kids to meet their maker. I have a plan ..."

Chapter 27

"I'm Mary Lightman. I was told that my son John is here."

The triage receptionist in the emergency department replied, "The doctor wants to talk with you. I'll let him know you're here."

John's mom stood at the reception desk, motionless, heart racing. She was a well-dressed lady, not pretentious, and always kept herself composed. Over the years, she learned to rely on her faith in times of trial, which in turn kept her emotions in check. Since she didn't know how serious John's injury was, she didn't presume the worst. While she waited patiently, she noticed a policeman with his back to her talking to a girl in the far corner of the waiting room.

A door flew open and a middle-aged doctor appeared before her. "Mrs. Lightman, your son John is in critical condition. He was stabbed in the abdomen and the internal bleeding will require immediate surgery. Although I'd prefer to fly him to St. Louis, I doubt he'd make the flight. I'm assembling a team to begin surgery as soon as possible. When it's over, I'll give you an update."

Before Mary could reply, a nurse shouted "Code blue in room 3!" They were losing vital signs on the boy, and the doctor was needed immediately. The doctor ran back through the door without saying another word.

Mary felt tears running down her face now that the gravity of the situation was sinking in. She turned around and noticed the policeman walking toward her. She recognized him as a coworker of her brother's at the police department. "Steve, what happened?" she asked.

"According to that girl over there, John came to the rescue of a girl being assaulted and got knifed."

Mary pointed toward Jennifer and asked, "Is that the girl he saved?"

"No, apparently she was a friend of his who was with him at the time. Do you recognize her?"

Mary looked pensive. "No, which is unusual because I thought I knew all his friends. Where's Scott?"

"Scott and I were answering a trespassing call at the sale barn when we got two emergency calls at the same time. He wanted to take the burglary while I took this one."

"He should be here."

"No, it's actually better that he's not here," replied Officer Steve.

"Why?"

"The girl over there is Jennifer Lawson. She's been indicted for the murder of Dana Keller. Scott would tear her to shreds if he was the arresting officer. I didn't find any evidence or witnesses at the scene of the crime to collaborate her story. It's still too early to make a judgment, but it's not looking good for her."

"Jennifer Lawson, she's the daughter of an old friend. She looks different now ... Scott should be on this case. Why did he take the burglary?"

"He had no idea John got hurt. We were checking out the sale barn trespass call, when the dispatcher announced two emergencies at the same time, an assault at the park and a break-in. We were just told that a woman was being assaulted at the park. Scott had no idea that John was involved. I guess you don't know yet, but he wanted to take the burglary because the dispatcher reported that it was your house that was being broken into. I need to go back to the park and look for evidence. John will be in my prayers."

"Thank you."

Mary turned her attention toward Jennifer, who was crying uncontrollably in the corner of the waiting room. She decided to walk over to Jennifer. As she got closer, she noticed Jennifer's eyes were closed and she was saying a rosary. She stared as Jennifer's fingers race through the beads wondering at the lightning speed at which the girl was praying.

It occurred to her that she might be looking at the murderess of her son. If so, she figured the girl must be bipolar or have some other illness. How could a young, slim girl overpower her son, who was muscular and strong, though? *Dear Lord, give me the grace to unconditionally love this young girl.*

"Jennifer, hi. I'm John's mom. Do you remember me?" she asked kindly.

Jennifer looked up and opened her eyes. They were bloodshot from crying. Tears were streaming from her eyes, but she didn't attempt to wipe them off. "I'm so sorry, Mrs. Lightman. It's entirely my fault. Please forgive me."

Before Mary could reply, she noticed her brother standing by her side in his police uniform.

Detective Scott Peterson began, "Miss Jennifer Lawson, you have the right to remain silent..."

Mary interrupted him, "Scott, this is not the time."

Scott turned to Mary. "Last week, Jennifer publicly stated that she hated John and at one point put her hands on his throat threatening to kill him."

He turned to Jennifer and continued, "Anything you say can and may be used against you ... "

Mary reiterated her objection by stressing, "Scott, this is not the time or the place!"

Scott ignored her plea again and attempted to proceed with his arrest.

Mary turned toward him and started jabbing him with her finger on his chest while accusing him a little too loudly, "Haven't you caused enough pain in others yet? Let it go, it wasn't your fault!" She then dropped into a chair, covered her face in her hands, and started crying.

Scott noticed a hospital security officer drawing his billy club, coming to his aid. The thought of the guard hitting his sister made him angry, so he stared down the guard with such indignation that the man quickly left the scene. Scott had a temper in which he earned the reputation of being someone you didn't want to mess with. It was evident that the security guard feared him just like everyone in the police department.

Scott decided it would be best to wait before arresting Jennifer. "Mary, I have to return to work. Call me when John can talk. I need to ask him some questions."

Mary replied, "If he survives, I will."

Scott ended with a chilling threat, "If he doesn't survive, Miss Lawson I'll request for you to be tried as an adult so that we can put you on death row."

Mary composed herself. She stood up and noticed that Jennifer had just sat there through the whole ordeal with her eyes closed, clenching rosary beads, crying her eyes out. She pitied her.

Sitting down on the couch next to Jennifer, Mary firmly held her trembling hand. "Jennifer, would you say a rosary with me for John? I'd appreciate it very much."

Without looking at Mary, Jennifer briefly collected herself from her sobbing to say one word. "Sure."

"Thanks, I'll lead, and you can say the responses. What mystery were you reflecting on?"

"I don't know, I was just saying the Hail Mary and Our Father."

It became clear to Mary that Jennifer didn't know how to pray and needed instruction. "Close your eyes and enter into a dialog with God, the Father, and Mary, His daughter. Talk to them like you're talking to me right now. As you talk to them, try to meditate on the life of Jesus. At the beginning it can be hard, but over time this prayer needs to become the joy of your heart. If you persevere, you'll find the rosary giving you peace in good times and comfort in times of sorrow."

Mary collected her thoughts and remembered it was Wednesday, so she began to lead the prayers of the Glorious Mysteries slowly and from the heart. Twenty minutes later, after the Hail Holy Queen, the pair found themselves much calmer.

The first thing Mary noticed was that Jennifer's hand was no longer trembling, nor was she crying uncontrollably. *That's a good sign.*

In an effort to keep the conversation light, Mary asked playfully, "I've noticed that John's been a little more chipper the past couple of days, and I suspected that a new girl was in his life. Are you the girl who's stolen his heart?"

Jennifer smiled while still looking down at her hands. "I don't think it is me because he told me that he hangs around me for charitable reasons."

Mary laughed at that thought. "Did John really say that? Trust me, he's not gaining a huge crown in heaven helping you out."

Jennifer smiled and finally looked at Mary. "Thanks. Could you ask God if John is going to be okay? I really need to know."

Mary grinned. "I would be happy to if it was only that easy."

"John seems to be able to do that."

Mary took a deep breath and looked into the distance. "John has a very special gift, but I'm afraid most us can't hear God in the same way he sometimes does."

"I don't understand. An hour ago I said my first prayer, and I heard God."

Mary looked at Jennifer inquisitively and said, "And what did God tell you?"

Tears started welling up in Jennifer's eyes. "You don't want to know."

"Does it concern John?"

"Yes."

Mary took a deep breath. John's mom politely replied, "Then I'd appreciate it if you told me."

"We heard a scream in the park. John told me to call for help as he ran toward the scream. After I called 911, I paused and said a short prayer, 'God, help John.' Then I heard a voice I never heard before say, 'If the blood of My Son is not sufficient for you to forgive, maybe John's blood will be sufficient.' I screamed 'no!' and then ran to find John. I saw him at the bottom of a hill approaching three men who were accosting a young girl. He just walked into the circle of the three guys holding his arms stretched out. He didn't even try to fight them. They let the girl run away and attacked him like a gang of wolves." Tears began to run down Jennifer's face as she relived the scene.

Just then she heard her cell phone ring. Jennifer said, "It's my mom. I really don't want to answer it because she'll make me come home. I need to stay here and make sure John is okay."

Mary gestured for Jennifer to hand her the phone.

An expression of fear came across Jennifer's face when she realized Mary's request. *Ever since the divorce, Mom blames everyone, including you, for her failed marriage.*

Mary patiently just held out her hand until Jennifer finally relented and placed the phone in her hands.

Mary answered the call. "Kate, hi, this is Mary Lightman. Jennifer's here with me at the hospital. ... Yes, she's okay. Apparently, John was stabbed trying to save a girl being assaulted in the park. He's in critical condition, in surgery as we speak, but it's uncertain whether he'll make it. Since my husband is out of the country, your daughter has been a great comfort to me. Would it be possible for her to stay here with me?"

Mary handed the phone to Jennifer.

"Hi, Mom. Yes, I want to stay. Thank you." Jennifer turned her phone off and looked at Mary. "Thank you very much. I want to be here for him."

"You're welcome. I meant those words I spoke to your mom. Just think how many mothers had to sit in this waiting room while their sons die a useless death. Maybe they die of a drug overdose or a car accident while drinking. You've given me the comfort of knowing that if John dies, he'll have died a good death. I'm indebted to you for sharing this with me. This is all very hard for me, but you've given me the only thing in the world that could offer me any comfort. Thank you."

Jennifer just nodded her head to politely acknowledge the kind words. "Today I went from the happiest day of my life to the worst. Just earlier this afternoon, John shared with me that he heard a voice in prayer telling him that he would set me free tonight."

Although Jennifer hoped to be free from unjustly being accused of murder, Mary suspected John was going to free her from her heavy chain of unforgiveness, which was crushing her. "The night's not over. Maybe he still will set you free. May I share a story with you?"

"Sure."

"About 50 years ago, there was a five-year-old boy riding home with his dad, who was a police officer. His dad, although not on duty at the time, assisted his fellow police officers who were having a shootout with some robbers. His dad told his son to stay put in the car. His son obeyed until a stray bullet hit the windshield, which prompted him to run to his father. When this father saw his boy running toward the line of fire, he ran out to save his son. A bullet killed his father. The young boy never forgave himself. When the boy was young, God poured out graces to help him forgive himself, which he rejected. Although the boy knew he should forgive himself, he chose not to. That boy later became a police officer and has spent his whole life putting away every bad guy he can find. He does his job without mercy. He is not motivated by justice but revenge. That boy's father was my father."

Jennifer put the pieces of the story together. "Detective Scott Peterson, your brother, was that boy?"

"Yes," replied Mary.

Jennifer came to Scott's defense, "Of course, it wasn't his fault."

"Self-pity is a form of pride rooted in self-love. It's very difficult for people to see, but unforgiveness is like a cancer that over time gnaws at the soul. It hardens the heart. Self-pity, like all sins, gives the soul a brief passing pleasure but makes the soul darker in the long run." After a brief pause Mary asked, "Who do you have a hard time forgiving?"

"It would be a complicated and long story."

"I can give you a couple of hours," Mary said smiling. "I'd find great comfort right now trying to help you through your unforgiveness and trying to complete the work John has begun in you."

Jennifer blurted out, "My ex-boyfriend dumped me for my best friend!"

Mary waited for Jennifer to offer more. *Jennifer just said her story was complicated.* After a minute of silence, Mary said, "If you don't want to talk to me about it, I'll leave you and go pray by myself. I can tell you're not being completely honest with me. I have a lot of questions about John that are bothering me. It pains me that I don't know the answers, but I think you do."

Jennifer sensed Mrs. Lightman was about to leave. "I'll answer any of your questions as truthfully as I can. I'm sorry. You're right, my unforgiveness is much deeper than that."

"Okay, we can try again. Why are you harboring unforgiveness?"

"I regret my abortion and have a lot of anger for those who talked me into it."

Mary took a deep breath and then said sincerely. "I'm very sorry for you." She decided it was best to get all the facts before offering any counseling. "You said your story was complicated."

"My life is a crazy mess lately. I don't know where to begin."

"Let's start with last Friday. John didn't return home till 2 a.m. Was he with you?"

"Yes, but it's not as bad as it seems. He did nothing wrong."

Mary replied kindly, "If he did nothing wrong, then there would be no problem telling me what you two did all night."

Jennifer briefly put her hands in her face. She then dropped her hands and took a deep breath.

It became obvious to Mary that this was the part that became complicated.

"We broke into my ex-boyfriend's house. We didn't actually break in because I knew where the hidden key was. The house was supposed to be vacant, but my ex came home early. We had to hide in his bedroom closet until he fell asleep, which took a long time because he'd just come down with the flu."

Mary could tell that Jennifer was becoming more tense and uncomfortable. Although her story seemed outlandish, why would she make up such a tale? In an effort to win her esteem back, Mary started giggling. "Did you find it a little humorous that you spent the night in your ex-boyfriend's closet?"

Jennifer smiled. "I do now, but at the time I was terrified."

"Let's use names so that I can follow your story a little better. What's the name of your ex?"

"Peter Wilson."

"The governor's son!?" Mary asked almost incredulously.

"Yep, that's him."

"Why did you and John break into the governor's home?"

"I don't know if you know this, but I am accused of murdering Dana Keller."

"I did know that."

"John read Dana's diary and discovered that it provided motives for four people who had reasons to murder her. Peter was one of the people, and Dana's dad was another."

"You need to share this with Scott. Although he is tough at times, he will pursue a criminal to the far ends of the earth."

"John tried to talk with Detective Peterson, but he didn't want to share the diary because it also provided a motive for me to kill Dana as well."

Mary replied, "So John thought the diary would be used against you if Scott saw it?"

Jennifer replied, "Yes."

"You haven't answered my question. Why break into the governor's home?"

"The diary mentioned that Dana put something in Peter's memorabilia box to blackmail him. John wanted to see what it was."

Mary asked, "What was it?"

"A picture that John described as being worthy to kill for."

"A picture of what?"

"Only John saw the picture, but he did say that it didn't involve me. It sounded like the governor would lose the election if it came out."

John's mom reflected on all that Jennifer disclosed. "So why would the diary indict you for the murder?"

"Dana pretended to be a close friend just to get dirt on the governor's family. When she learned I was pregnant, she was paid a bonus to talk me into an abortion, which she insisted Peter pay for." Jennifer continued after wiping away a new tear, "Dana used the blackmail photo to make Peter break up with me so that she could begin a fling with him."

"I'm sorry you suffered that." After pausing for a moment, Mary continued, "I got a call from school today. Apparently, John didn't show up. Were you with him?"

"I was with him after school let out. He told me that earlier in the day he was at church praying."

After a pause, Mary asked, "Why did he feel the need skip school to pray?"

"He said that yesterday afternoon he was attacked by demons, and he needed to regroup spiritually."

"Where did this spiritual attack occur?"

"In Dana's bedroom," Jennifer confessed sheepishly.

"Why was he in Dana's bedroom?"

"To get her laptop, which has information to help us figure out who murdered Dana."

"Did he get it?"

"Yes."

Mary wondered whether Jennifer was getting confused, so she stated, "I read that Dana's house was broken into on Sunday night, but you said John broke in on Monday night."

"The Sunday night attempted robbery was probably by a man who's hanging out with Peter. John broke in on Monday night and found the evidence everyone was looking for. The man who tried to break in Sunday is probably also the man who broke into my house yesterday while John was breaking into Dana's."

"Your house got broken into yesterday! Mine got broken into this evening. Do you know who broke into mine?"

"It could have been one of a couple of suspects."

"I'm sorry, but I think Scott needs to know this."

"John planned on telling him tonight. He said Scott would be dropping by his house."

Mary asked, "Why would Scott be dropping by my house tonight?"

"This is going to get even more complicated. Scott was going to question John why he was trespassing at the sale barn tonight."

Mary started doubting Jennifer's story. *Maybe she is a psycho.* "Why would John trespass at the sale barn?"

"Dana's diary indicated that her dad was smuggling drugs on his cattle trailers. John knew the cameras would catch his car driving on the lot but didn't care. He needed to take pictures of a stock trailer parked in the lot. It sounded like John had all the evidence he needed for Scott to make an arrest."

"I'm sorry. I believed you up to the drug smuggling operation." Mary got out her cell phone and called Scott.

"Scott, hi. It's Mary."

"How's John?"

"We haven't heard any news yet, but I'll let you know when I hear something. I heard you responded to a trespassing incident at the sale barn tonight. What can you tell me about it?"

"Why do you ask?"

"Was John there? I need to know."

"Yes, I looked at the surveillance camera and noticed John's car. He looked into a stock trailer and left. I didn't tell anyone that John was the intruder. I'd planned on dropping by your house tonight and discussing the situation with him personally."

"Thanks. That answers my question. I'll call when I know anything about John. Good-bye."

Mary turned to Jennifer, "Please accept my apologies for not believing you. You confided in me, and I feel that I made a mistake in not trusting you."

Jennifer smiled, "John has won me the grace to be able to forgive. I forgive you and everyone." After a brief pause, she added sadly, "I don't think I can forgive myself, though, for the pain I've caused John and the danger I put him in. As you can tell by my soap opera life, I'm not worth it."

Mary's disposition changed as she sat up straight. In a serious tone she replied, "You did NOT cause John's pain, nor did those three men. He freely gave his life for you!" Mary let those words sink in for a moment.

She noticed Jennifer beginning to cry when she added, "Please, look at me." Once Jennifer looked at Mary, she continued, "You're not going to look into my eyes, while my son is struggling for his life, and tell me my son suffered in vain for you, are you?"

Jennifer sat there frozen, not knowing what to say. It pained her to look at John's mom suffering, but she felt like she had no option.

Mary started nodding her head no as she continued, "No, I can tell that you're a good person and wouldn't do that. You must forgive yourself right now. This is your moment of grace. If you don't do it right now, I fear what kind of person you'll be fifty years from now."

Mary knew that Jennifer didn't know what she needed to do to forgive herself, so she helped her, "Look at me and repeat this back to me if you can mean it. 'Thank you for the blood your son shed for me. I needed those graces to change. From this point forward, I'll forget the past and live to be the child of God I'm called to be.' "

Jennifer looked into Mary's eyes and repeated her words. "Thank you for the blood your son shed for me. I needed those graces to change. From this point forward, I'll forget the past and live to be the child of God I'm called to be." Fresh tears streamed down Jennifer's eyes as she finished.

"Now, that wasn't so hard, was it?" Mary said kindly. *What pain we must have caused the Blessed Virgin Mary!*

Jennifer vehemently disagreed, "What do you mean? To look into your kind eyes and thank you for the blood your son shed for me! That was the hardest thing I ever had to do in my life!"

"I'm glad you found it hard because it wasn't easy for me, either. I'm glad that you're accepting his sacrifice. The devil will try to fill your mind up with thoughts of self-pity from time to time. You must reject them. I hope you'll never forget this moment. Even though it will cost me great agony, I hope my son will die if that's what it takes for you to forgive yourself. You need to. By the grace of God, live from this moment on as a new person; a person who forgives because she has been forgiven."

"I want to. I wanted to before the stabbing, but I was afraid of John's world. Now, I only fear living in my old world. It has caused me and those around me so much misery."

◆ ◆ ◆

After some time, Jennifer began to worry about all the evidence sitting in John's car. That worried Jennifer. John mentioned that he didn't care if the sale barn camera identified him because he was about to surrender it all to Scott this evening. The unexpected stabbing complicated things. Berryville was a small town, and soon everyone would know John's fate. Although the thought of walking alone, in the dark of the night, to John's car terrified her, she knew she had to do it. She excused herself and proceeded on her mission to retrieve the evidence that cost Dana her life.

Chapter 28

The next day, Jennifer was beyond elated when she saw John's eyes open. "Hey, sleeping beauty!" she teased.

"You're a sight for sore eyes. Actually, everything feels sore right now."

Jennifer smiled. "Your mom just stepped out. She'll be back in a minute. She'll be ecstatic to see you awake. We've talked for hours. You're so lucky to have a mom like her."

"I'm glad you two hit it off." John looked around the hospital room. "What day is it?"

"It's Thursday afternoon. You were stabbed last night."

A faint ring came from Jennifer's handbag. She picked up her cell phone and noticed Allison was calling her. "It's just Allie."

"Take it."

Jennifer hesitated but then answered. She sat on the edge of John's bed and stared at John as she talked. It was apparent that she had little interest in talking with Allison.

After a few minutes of small talk, Jennifer's interest in the conversation changed. "So Peter is asking you out, and you told him that I had to give you my okay. Alli, you're going to be an old maid if you keep this up. You have my blessing."

John, are you listening, because I've forgiven Peter?

Another minute of conversation passed. Jennifer ended with, "Don't concern yourself with how Peter broke up with me because Dana pressured him into it. He didn't act on his own free will. Allie, I wish you and Peter all the happiness in this world. Bye."

Jennifer triumphantly looked at John. "I've forgiven Peter, Dana, and myself. Most importantly, I've asked God for His forgiveness. I need to thank you for this."

John tried to smile. "I'm very proud of you, but could you please do me a favor?"

"Sure, anything."

"Don't leave the hospital until the case is solved. You might have just told Peter that you know he was being blackmailed."

Jennifer buried her face in her hands. "I can't believe I did that. I wanted to put Peter in a good light to show I forgave him. I'm a complete screw-up, forgive me."

John welcomed the thought of Jennifer being stuck in the hospital. "You're forgiven. Since I enjoy your company," John paused and raised his eyebrows, "most of the time, it will be okay with me to have you stuck in the hospital."

"Thank you," Jennifer hesitated and grinned, "I think."

John grinned back.

Jennifer walked over to the window. "I'm so happy you'll be okay. You don't know how much you mean to me. If something happened to you because of me, I don't know how I could live with myself."

"Why do you believe my injury has anything to do with you?"

"God told me."

John joked, "If you think you're hearing voices, then maybe you need to see a doctor with a couch."

Jennifer laughed. "I deserved that."

At John's pleading, Jennifer shared with him the park episode in which God revealed to her the sacrifice John made on her behalf. Since he knew there was no other way she could have deduced the intent of his actions, he was convinced that God had spoken to her. *She has no idea what a grace she has received!*

Silently, John thanked God for answering his prayer.

Jennifer got excited. "Your mom helped me figure out Dana's riddle! We had a lot of fun working on it." Jennifer pulled out a piece of paper from her purse and read.

Oh, Sorceress who feeds me with stardust
You serve a master who's the prince of this earth,
Oh, Sorceress promises yours truly so many things my heart delights,
Who can bring snow in July is a friend to behold!
Leunam, Leunam, Leunam, is my backward snowman,
If diamonds can be found in ruffs, then snow can be found in dung,
Paternal secrets provide the key to power and control.

"Someone she refers to as a 'sorceress' was feeding her with 'stardust,' which is a synonym for heroin. This 'sorceress' has a master who's the prince of this earth, which of course is Satan. 'Snow in July' refers to her big stash of white heroin she got in July. It was secretly stored in the manure of the stock trailer. Leunam is the name 'Manuel' spelled backwards. That is why she referred to him as the 'backward snowman.' Learning of her dad's drug smuggling business is what is meant by 'paternal secrets'."

"Here's the unencrypted version:

There is a 'sorceress' who feeds Dana with heroin
Satan is the master of this 'sorceress' who supplies her drugs
Officer Manuel supplied Dana with a load of heroin in July,
which was hidden in cow manure
The knowledge of my dad's secret drug business will give me
power and control

"You're better than Sherlock Homes! You figured out an important part of the puzzle."

Jennifer beamed at his compliment.

John continued. "Jennifer, let's talk about the murder scene. I sense real danger for us right now. We have little time to figure this all out."

Jennifer replied mockingly yet with a worried tone. "You don't have to worry about being in danger because your uncle just assigned a police officer to guard your hospital room."

John gave her an inquisitive look. He knew by the tone of her reply there was more to her comment than she was letting on. "He thinks one of the gang members will be after me?"

"Not really." Jennifer wondered if he could figure out her riddle.

"The sooner this morphine wears off, the better." John rubbed his eyes. "Don't tell me our friend Officer Manuel is standing guard."

"Bingo! Apparently, someone wrote a lot of graffiti on your living room walls last night that were full of death threats—someone who must have known that you and your mom were at the hospital. Anyway, Scott decided to appoint a guard for you. Officer Manuel volunteered because he said he needed extra money."

John's pulse raced. "The security cameras at the sale barn must have given me away. This isn't good."

"I tried to talk your uncle out of stationing Officer Manuel as a guard, but it didn't go very well." Jennifer's shoulders sank dejectedly. "Your uncle still thinks I was alone at the park trying to get to your heart … but with a knife. I might be on death row right now if it wasn't for your mom."

John gave her a devilish smile. "If you want Uncle Scott to know the truth, you better be nice to me!"

A mortified look came across Jennifer face. "This isn't funny!"

John laughed, "I'll straighten the matter out with him right now. Can you have my mom get a hold of Uncle Scott ASAP?"

"Interesting you'd suggest that because your mom just stepped out about five minutes ago to call him. She left the room so that she wouldn't disturb your sleep." Jennifer became excited. "I forgot to mention your home was burglarized last night at the same time you visited the sale barn."

"Interesting." John smiled, "Too bad for him I brought Dana's stuff on our stake out last night. We need to wrap Dana's murder up because from the sounds of it, Dana's dad, maybe Peter, and/or your secret admirer have figured out that I have Dana's computer and phone. This also means that they know I know too much."

Jennifer walked over to a beautiful bouquet and smelled a flower. "What can I do?"

John ignored her question and asked, "Who are the flowers from?"

"The card says 'Jill and Family.' "

"That was nice of her. Let's get started." John pushed the button on his bed remote and moved to a sitting position. "See the knife left on my lunch tray? Please lay on the floor and position the knife exactly as you found it in Dana."

Jennifer's smile left her face. She took a deep breath and did as he requested.

"Are you sure she was stabbed on the right side."

"Positive."

"You said there was a book near her body. Where do you think she was reading it before she was stabbed?"

Jennifer pointed to a spot just behind her. "I think she was sitting in her bedroom chair."

"Now sit in the chair and pretend you are Dana reading a book. How would she position it?"

Jennifer sat in the chair behind her and held up a book close to her face. "She read like this."

"Are you sure she held the book that high and close to her face?"

"She didn't see well and hated wearing glasses. She would read a book about six inches from her face."

"Okay. Now position the knife the way it would have entered her body."

Jennifer positioned the knife just under the right rib cage. "I guess it would have been like this."

"Since you pulled out the knife, try to remember very carefully—was it positioned up or down, left or right?"

Jennifer thought for a second. "The knife might have been positioned slightly down and a little toward the outside."

"I know who did it and why!" John looked up and saw his mom standing at the doorway. She appeared to be in shock. "Mom, it's okay. I asked Jennifer to recount Dana's crime scene."

Jennifer left the chair and returned the knife to the hospital tray.

"It's not that." Mary moved to his bedside.

Jennifer greeted her with a smile, which wasn't returned.

Mary nervously asked, "Son, how are you doing?"

Sensing something was amiss with his mom, John replied, "I was doing fine until you walked in. What's wrong?"

Mary walked over to the TV and turned on the news. The breaking news story of the day was the abortion love triangle scandal among Jennifer, Peter, and Dana. The paperwork for the abortion was flashed on the screen documenting the governor's son paying for an abortion. The newsman mentioned the irony in Peter Wilson speaking at a pro-life event just days after paying his lover, Jennifer Lawson, for an abortion.

The breaking story shifted to report on the Lightman family. It was announced that since the murder, the son of long-time campaign aide Mary Lightman has been in a romantic involvement with the accused murderess, Jennifer Lawson. A picture of John holding Jennifer's head in his hands at the park was flashed over the screen.

Just before breaking for a commercial, the anchor announced that Governor Wilson's campaign had been postponed until the press briefing tomorrow at 11 a.m. in his hometown of Berryville.

God knows the truth. Do what is right and be at peace. Jennifer shot John a fake smile. "Why am I always the last to know things? Did you hear? We're an item."

Mary found no humor in Jennifer's joke.

John looked at Jennifer. "That picture was taken at the park by your secret admirer." John noticed his mom's uneasiness. "That picture isn't what it seems."

Mary didn't reply.

Jennifer walked over to turn down the volume. "I'm sorry, but the TV is disturbing my peace. You guys will have to just read the captions because I've heard enough."

John glanced at Jennifer and noticed that she was a changed person. The anger in her was gone. In the past she would have offered an intense emotional response to such slanderous accusations. He suspected that she had finally stepped into his world. *How else could she remain so peaceful?*

Just as Jennifer was turning down the volume, she noticed the governor's opponent, Charlie Biton, offering his comments on the affair. His response was one of shock regarding the hypocrisy of a fellow politician. Jennifer was surprised to recognize the woman standing behind Charlie. "I met that lady standing behind Mr. Biton at Dana's. Who is she?"

Mary looked closely at the TV. "That's Eleanor Smith, Biton's campaign manager."

John became interested. "Tell me everything you know about her."

"About a month ago, I saw her walking out of Dana's house to her car. Her facial features are so distinct I don't think I'd ever forget her. Then a week later, the door to Dana's house was open when I popped in, and I found that lady in Dana's bedroom. Both were uncomfortable with me dropping in unexpectedly. I noticed an envelope of cash on the dresser, but I didn't inquire about it. It was a strange meeting because Dana never introduced me. I don't think Dana liked her much."

John listened intently. "Why would you say that Dana didn't like her?"

"Several days later, I asked Dana who she was. She just said, 'she's a witch.' "

John became very excited. "Witch is synonymous with sorceress. Where is Uncle Scott?"

Mary looked at her son. "He's undercover at a stakeout and can't be reached. The police chief thought he would be home around midnight. When we last talked this morning, he told me that he was planning on visiting you tomorrow around 8 a.m. He can't wait to talk to you."

John smiled. "Me, too. Mom, don't believe the news. It's all lies. Tomorrow I'll explain everything. Just in case I don't get the chance to tell him personally, please tell him Jennifer had nothing to do with my stabbing, and she's innocent regarding Dana's murder."

John's mom froze as the full force of his last sentence sunk in.

Jennifer heard a phone ringing. "Mrs. Lightman, your phone."

"Thanks, Jennifer."

Mary pressed the answer button and saw the caller ID as Governor Wilson's campaign headquarters. "Hi, Tim. I'm so sorry."

Tim was unusually distant to Mary. Given the present scandal, she was sad to know the five years of volunteering on behalf of the governor didn't win her any slack. Although it was apparent the race was over, it was protocol in time of scandal that all parties involved not talk with the press until the strategy room decided how to respond. "The press secretary wants you and your son to decline making any comments on the scandal until further notice."

Mary looked distraught. "All right." Mary noticed Jennifer gesturing for the phone. "Jennifer Lawson is sitting beside me and would like to speak to you."

Jennifer placed the phone to her ear. "Hi! Please tell Governor Wilson that I'm very sorry for all the pain he must be feeling. I had nothing to do with leaking this scandal to the press, and I wish him the best."

Tim was silent on the other end.

Her response to the cold shoulder treatment was "Thank you." Jennifer noticed John gesturing for the phone. "Hold on, it appears that Mary's son, John, would like to speak with you."

Jennifer's subtle body language revealed to John that she was stiffed on the phone. John took the phone and winked at Jennifer. In a tone of authority, he began, "I have a message for the governor that is for his ears only. I have documented proof that Eleanor Smith orchestrated this whole scandal. The level of proof I will be able to provide will not be questioned.

Have Governor Wilson, Peter, and Gene Simpson drop by my hospital room tomorrow at 8:30 a.m. sharp . It will make the governor's day. It's imperative that this conversation remains a secret until I talk with the governor. If this request is breached, I'll destroy the evidence and the governor will go down in flames. Understood?"

A timid voice replied, "Understood."

Mary grabbed the phone from John. "Tim, I don't know what John's talking about, but I assure you his word is good." She decided to just end the call before any questions could be asked.

Chapter 29

"Hi, Belinda, this is your favorite snake calling."

"Who said you were my favorite snake?"

"You said you like powerful ones. Right now, I think of myself as a King snake."

"Too bad there is no such thing as a Queen snake, or I'd take that title."

"I'm glad there isn't because you like snakes, but I don't."

"What do you like?"

"Young, pretty campaign interns."

Belinda laughed. "Working in politics has shown me that everywhere I look I see two things, snakes and pretty girls. The only thing is that the snakes survive the test of time, whereas the pretty girls come and go; or more accurately, they're thrown out like trash."

Jim expressed false empathy, "What you say is sad but true. It's the price that must be paid for liberating women from the shackles of motherhood."

Belinda felt unsettled by his comment because she wanted to be a wife and have kids one day. Of course, these dreams took second seat to wanting the liberty to be wild for now. The dichotomy of feelings between Jim and her was upsetting. "So you aren't going to correct my perceptions of politics?"

"Only to add that not all snakes are created equal. There are snakes, and there are powerful snakes." Jim sensed something amiss and decided to change the subject. "What are the polls showing?"

Belinda welcomed the change of subject. "We were down by two points the past five days. Since the scandal broke, things are looking up. Although it's unofficial, our polls are now showing a seven-point swing overnight, which gives us a five-point gain. This momentum shift is just the beginning. Our pollster told the office an hour ago that every time this has previously happened at this point in the race, it has meant a landslide victory. People are getting out the champagne already. I wish you were here."

"Why? Do you want to see a drunk snake?"

Belinda laughed. "How come I suspect that you might have had something to do with the governor's scandal that's breaking?"

In a false pretense of innocence, Jim replied, "How could you think such a thing? Can you please transfer me to The Witch?"

Jim turned on his recorder before Eleanor began to speak.

"I guess you saw the news."

"It looks like the whole country saw the news. I hear Biton is doing better in the polls now."

"Unless your friend John Lightman causes a problem, the victory is ours!" Eleanor inquired, "Did you get the laptop and phone?"

"Last night, I went through John's house, and it wasn't there. He knew I'd be looking for it because on his desk was a note written in big print saying, 'Dana's computer and phone are not here.' I still ransacked his room anyway."

Eleanor groaned.

Jim confidently continued. "I have some news on John. He got stabbed last night and is laid up in the hospital. I bugged his hospital room this morning by placing a listening device in some flowers. But there's bad news. He knows the whole scam and is going to give Governor Wilson all the evidence to vindicate him from the scandal tomorrow morning. The good news, though, is that he revealed that he hasn't shared the evidence with anyone else."

"Good job. You need to see that he doesn't see the light of day tomorrow. Is the girl despairing yet?"

"I'm afraid not."

"She will tomorrow when she mourns John's dead body."

Chapter 30

Later in the evening, Jill popped her head into John's hospital room and was greeted by Jennifer's warm smile.

Jennifer whispered, "He's sleeping."

Jill tiptoed in carrying a bouquet of white spider mums and Jennifer's overnight bag.

Jennifer gave Jill a puzzled look as she took her flowers and set them on the dresser with the other arrangement. "Let's talk in the bathroom."

Jill leaned comfortably against the bathroom sink. "How's he doing?"

"He's in critical condition but improving. The prognosis looks good."

Jennifer peaked through the crack in the door and checked on John. "How did you make it past the guard?"

"What guard?"

"John's uncle placed a guard at the door because of some death threats."

"I didn't see a guard."

"Doesn't surprise me, he's only there about half the time." Jennifer grabbed the suitcase. "Thanks for packing me an overnight bag. I hope I didn't put you out too much."

"Oh no, glad to help. There are about a dozen reporters camped outside your house waiting for you to come home. They mobbed me, and even though I showed them my driver's license, they still didn't believe I wasn't you. I had to sneak out your bedroom window to get away from them."

Jennifer pushed up her hair in playful arrogance. "I'm famous."

"Then I never want to be famous!" Jill said sternly. "How are you doing?"

"Really good!" Jennifer again peeked out the door. "I can't wait till this mess is over. Tomorrow, this chapter in my life will be behind me."

Jill grinned mischievously. "I can't help noticing how you stare at John. How is your knight in shining armor?"

Jennifer gave Jill a flabbergasted look. "Don't you ever think about anything other than boys?"

If that's not the kettle calling the pot black. Jill only returned a polite smile.

Jennifer decided to defend herself against the accusation. "There is a reason I keep looking at him. John's life is in danger. His mom and I take turns watching him." Jennifer then conceded her true feelings. "Yes, my knight in shining armor is doing well if you have to know. He likes me a lot."

Jill questioned, "A lot?"

Jennifer beamed, "A lot!"

Jill teased her, "Like jump in front of a moving train for you 'a lot'?"

"He already did that for me." Jennifer went on to explain the park episode, describing how John offered himself up to win the graces for her conversion.

Jill was overwhelmed by the whole story and how God spoke to her. Although John frequently amazed her with his level of faith, this story topped them all. Jill nervously joked, "I guess you have to forgive everyone now."

Jennifer nodded yes, "I know I've been forgiven, and I want to show the world I've forgiven people, too. Next week, let's hang out on your dock and chat."

"I'd love that. Was it hard to forgive me?"

Jennifer teased, "For which sin, dumping me a year ago or giving my guy two bouquets?"

Jill protested. "I don't know what you mean. I only brought this bouquet."

Jennifer's happy disposition changed to one of fright. She raises her index finger to her mouth to beckon silence. The two tiptoed to the window where several flower arrangements were resting.

She pulled out the card that read "Jill and Family."

Jill looked at the card and flowers and then nodded no.

Jennifer looked around the flowers and noticed a transmitting device stuffed in the artificial moss and pointed it out to Jill.

The two walked back into the bathroom.

Jill was shocked. "Do you want me to take the flowers with 'ears' home with me when I leave?"

Jennifer thought for a moment. "When John wakes up, I'll tell him that his flowers have a 'bad bug' and see what he wants to do about it. Since whoever planted the bug doesn't know we know, maybe we can use it to our advantage."

"You look worried."

"I am a little because the conversation we had here earlier today would be enough to have John killed for."

"How about you?"

"John has protected me. The person listening would understand that John is the only threat."

Jill became alarmed. "Let's tell the policeman at the door."

Jennifer grabbed Jill forcibly by the shoulders. "You must promise me you will NOT do that."

Jill was very surprised but surrendered the idea. "I promise, but why?"

Jennifer let Jill go. "It's complicated, but tomorrow morning it will all be over. There is a slight chance that you're in danger. Just to be safe, it might be best if you were out of the picture. Forgive me."

Jennifer took Jill by the hand and walked her in front of the flowers. "Jill, I saw the text you wrote John last night. I thought I could trust you, but you've shown your true colors."

Jill protested her innocence, "I think there's a mistake."

Jennifer interrupted her and continued her assault, "John's my boyfriend, not yours. I never want to see you again. Just GO!"

Jill caught on to what Jennifer was doing. Jennifer set up a mock fight to protect Jill. As the two silently hugged at the door, Jill whispered in Jennifer's ear, "You didn't have to do that. I wanted to be here for you!"

"I know, but I don't think I could handle seeing two people I care about being hurt on my behalf."

Chapter 31

Later that night, Mary listened to the monotonous beeping of the heart monitor relentlessly piercing the stillness of John's hospital room. The annoying noise was a comforting reminder that John's vitals were okay. Even with this reassuring sound, Mary still sat in the blackness of the night waiting in fear.

Although at first she didn't comprehend the danger her son was in, now that she caught Officer Manuel on two separate occasions trying to sneak into John's room, she acutely perceived the danger to be real. The first occurrence happened a little after midnight. When she came out of the bathroom, she caught him hovering over John. The second time was an hour ago at 2 a.m.

Each unwelcomed visit by Officer Manuel was immediately met with Mary pressing John's emergency call button. Although on each occasion a nurse rushing into the room defused the danger, the last one included a warning that if she pressed the button again she would be asked to leave the hospital. She regretted not joining Jennifer's protest when Scott announced that Officer Manuel was going to be standing guard.

The clock read 3 a.m. *Scott will be here in five hours.*

Officer Manual ignored clear instructions not to enter the room. He pretended not to fully understand English while justifying his actions as part of doing his job. Mary knew he was lying but also knew there was little she could do until she talked with her brother. Her call to his cell went unanswered. She wished her brother was with her right now, but she had no alternative other than waiting and guarding her son while he slept.

Mary sat wondering how she would respond if Officer Manuel tried to enter John's room again. The thought of being asked to leave the hospital was unthinkable. The worse part of the situation was that not only Officer Manuel knew that Mary might be asked to leave the hospital, but that he had won the esteem of the hospital staff. When no solution came to mind on how she should react if Officer Manuel entered John's room, she decided to resume praying.

Her prayers were distracted with the thought that maybe she should wake up Jennifer, who had been sleeping soundly through the first two intrusions. She dispelled the thought because it was apparent that Jennifer would not be of much help. Although neither of them slept much the night before, Jennifer didn't sleep the previous night as well because of the burglary at her home.

Dear Lord, what do I do if Officer Manuel walks into this room again? Once again, her prayer seemed unanswered.

Fear rose in her as she noticed the hospital room door begin to open. It was too late to wake up Jennifer. Her hand grabbed the emergency call button and waited.

Her fear subsided when she noticed a hospital nurse walk into the room holding a tray. He was a young man around thirty. He whispered, "Time for his medication."

Mary shot him a smile as she noticed that he was unsure where to set the tray down. "What medication is he getting?"

The nurse picked up a needle and began injecting John's IV bottle. "It's time for another dose of morphine."

Before she could protest, the nurse was gone. She was furious. She heard the doctor agree to John's wishes of no morphine.

Mary aggressively shook Jennifer. Once half awake, she was

ordered to stand guard. Mary pitied her for her severe sleep deprivation, but this situation warranted an immediate response.

Mary opened John's hospital room door. The deserted hallway afforded her the opportunity to walk up to the nurse's station. She wondered where Officer Manuel was. Every couple of steps, she turned her head to look back toward John's door to ensure his safety. Since the hallway was deserted, she began to worry that paranoia was setting in.

An older nurse was sitting at her desk filling out paperwork. "May I help you?"

"I'd like to talk to the nurse in charge."

"That would be me. I'm Susan, how can I help you?"

Mary briefly returned her glance at John's door and noticed the hallway still deserted. "I would like to know why my son's request of no morphine was not honored. I heard the doctor agreed to comply with his wishes."

Susan turned to a colleague two stations over. "Samantha, you have the Lightman boy on your shift, don't you?"

A recent graduate of nursing school walked over to the two ladies. "Yes, he's my patient."

"Mrs. Lightman is inquiring why her son is getting morphine. She claims that the doctor didn't require it."

Samantha looked at Mary. "That's true. The doctor told me the patient didn't want any morphine. I was to administer it to him only if I noticed any visible pain. Your son John hasn't received any morphine tonight."

Mary glanced back to John's door. The hall was still clear. "A nurse just injected John's IV bottle with morphine. I saw him."

"That's not possible because I'd be the only one authorized to administer any medicine to him." Samantha gave Susan a worried look, especially since a guard had been assigned to watch his room.

"Remove the IV," demanded the head nurse as she picked up the hospital phone. "Code red! This is Susan Beyer, Head Nurse, I'm requesting an immediate emergency hospital lockdown."

While the head nurse explained the situation to hospital security, Mary took the opportunity to call Scott. This time he answered. She told him that an attempt on John's life was just made. Scott promised to be there in five minutes.

Samantha ran back to the nurse's station. "Code blue room 105."

Mary's heart sank. Room 105 was John's room.

"Mrs. Lightman, please go to the security station located at the front doors of the hospital and assist them in identifying the nurse you saw. I'll let them know you're on your way. I have to go."

When Mary reached the elevators, she looked back to notice doctors and nurses rushing into John's room. *Dear Lord, give me strength.*

Moments later, Mary introduced herself to the two guards standing at the main hospital door.

"Mam, the hospital is locked down. If the culprit's still here, he won't get out."

Mary inquired, "Did a man in his thirties walk out in the past five minutes? He was dressed as a nurse."

The younger guard replied. "I've been sitting at this desk since midnight, and I don't recall a person fitting that description walking out the door."

The ding of the elevator caught Mary's attention. She saw the man who pretended to be the nurse walking out of the elevator. Although he had changed into street clothes, she was sure it was him. She pointed her finger at him and screamed, "That's him!"

The suspect began to flee down the hall with the hospital security guards in pursuit. The lone janitor correctly assessed the situation and tripped him up with his mop as he attempted to pass. The suspect did a face plant on the tile floor, and moments later the two hospital security guards jumped on top of him.

Sirens could be heard getting louder and louder until they were at the front entrance. Scott came running down the hallway in orange pin-striped pajamas with a pistol strapped around his waist. Something about his demeanor demanded respect regardless of the garb he was wearing.

Mary was leaning against the wall trying to hold back her tears. "Scott, he was the one who just tried to kill John."

Scott looked at the two guards who were struggling to stay on top of the squirming man. "Good job boys, I'll take it over from here." Scott leaned over and placed his left hand under the suspect's right arm pit and grabbed the right wrist with his other hand. Once the suspect's arm was fully extended, Scott turned the arm backwards a half turn. A loud cursing scream ensued.

Scott smiled and looked at the hospital guards panting with exhaustion. "You guys can get off him and take a break."

The two men clumsily complied and watched in admiration at how Scott could so easily manhandle the impostor.

Scott looked down at the suspect, while still applying painful pressure and asked, "I'm going to have you stand against the wall so that I can search you. Can I expect your cooperation?"

The suspect just continued to moan in pain.

"I expected you to say yes." Scott smiled and tweaked his arm another slight turn.

The fresh agonizing pain almost made the suspect pass out. Although the scream was unintelligible, there was no doubt to the onlookers he tried to say yes.

Scott assumed his sister wasn't approving of his heavy-handed arresting techniques, so he decided to proceed with the arrest. "I will take your response as a yes." Scott let go of the suspect's right arm, which just dangled in duress.

Scott then firmly grabbed a handful of the suspect's hair and started forcibly lifting him up. The man squealed with new pain. As soon as he was lifted halfway up, Scott issued his command. "I want you to stand up and face the wall."

Once the suspect was standing, Scott started kicking the suspect's feet apart. After the third kick, he decided to voice the command. "Spread your feet."

The young security guard quickly informed him. "Detective Peterson, he tried to grab something in is left pocket, but I never let him get it."

"Thank you. I'm going to search you now. If you even flinch, I'll assume you're resisting arrest, and I promise you, you'll be sorry." Scott started padding the suspect down. When he got to the chest, he pulled out an audio recorder. "I bet there's something on here that he wanted to erase. Great job not letting him erase it."

Just then, back-up police officers showed up. Scott barked some orders. "Handcuff this man and read him his rights. Give him a chair in the interrogation room. I'm going to go home and change. I'll be at the station shortly. My new friend and I have a lot to chat about."

"Yes sir," responded the officer.

Scott picked up the suspect's duffle bag and opened it up. He saw a nurse's uniform, a cell phone, and hospital shoes. He thumbed through the bag a little more and came across a small vial labeled 'cyanide.' Scott shook his head no. *I hope John's okay.* He ripped off the badge from the man's shirt and handed it to the security guard. "Run this badge in your computer and tell me if it's legit."

The security guard took one look at the badge and replied, "I don't have to run it through our computer; I can tell you that it's a fake just looking at it."

"Thank you." Scott turned to Mary. "How's John?"

"When I left, I saw doctors and nurses running into the room. I'm not sure."

"I guess we might have the guy who killed Dana." Scott was relieved to know justice would be done.

Mary looked at the suspect being led away in handcuffs. Although she desperately wanted to check on John, she knew she had to talk with her brother first. "Can I talk with you alone?"

The two walked down the hall and stopped at a deserted lounge. "John needs to talk with you. It seems as though there might be two or three people wanting to kill him. One of them killed Dana, and he knows who. Apparently, he's been helping Jennifer Lawson prove her innocence. In doing so, he discovered the information that Dana was using to blackmail these people. Now, these two or three people want to see John dead."

"I'm glad I stationed Officer Manuel there."

"Officer Manuel is one of the people who wants John dead."

"Are you sure?"

"Yes. John has evidence that he's part of a Mexican drug-smuggling operation." Mary noticed that Scott was becoming angry. She knew his anger would lead to irrational decisions and quietly said a prayer for him.

"I smelled a rat when the chief hired him, but he wouldn't listen to me." Scott started shaking his head in a fury.

"Scott, is it possible that you could keep the guy you just arrested and Officer Manuel at the station without allowing them to make phone calls until you talk with John?"

"For a couple of hours, sure, but why?"

"John was adamant yesterday that everything was to be kept a secret until he talked with you."

"We can keep this a secret for a few hours. Let's go check on John and chat with Officer Manuel."

Once in the elevator, Scott apologized to Mary for not listening to John when he said he had some evidence to share. "Mary, I could kick myself. If I'd listened to John, maybe none of this would have happened."

Mary graciously accepted his apology and assured him that this wasn't his fault.

Scott and Mary got off the elevator and immediately went up to the nurse's station. Mary glanced down the hall and noticed that Officer Manuel was now sitting in his chair. Mary caught the attention of John's nurse. "How is he?"

"He's doing fine." The young nurse looked down in embarrassment, "When I removed the IV, I accidently knocked off the EKG clip from his finger and the machine went dead. I panicked and called 'code blue.' I'm sorry for the worry I must have caused you."

Mary was relieved. "Don't worry about it. Thank you for taking care of my son."

Justice needed to be administered, so Scott interrupted them. "Let's chat with Officer Manuel."

The two walked toward John's room. Scott appeared calm but felt silly in his bedtime clothing. Although he didn't fear anyone would have the courage to laugh at him, he knew the reporters would arrive soon and didn't want to be featured in any of the newspapers.

Scott put on a serious look. "Carlos, I need you at the police station with me when I do my interrogation of John's would-be killer. I'm disappointed that you'd allow this to happen."

Carlos began to protest.

Scott was taken back at his insubordination. He commanded, "Now! You'll ride with me in my car. Let's go."

Carlos knew he had no other option. The consequences of not listening to a direct command from Scott would cost him dearly. Although he wanted to call Tim to apprise him of the situation, Scott made sure he didn't get the chance. Back at the station, Scott strip-searched Carlos and found a bottle of arsenic. When Carlos was placed in the holding cell, he started confessing the whole operation in hopes of gaining a plea bargain.

Chapter 32

The clock read 7:45 a.m.

Jennifer peeked in the room and noticed John was sitting up with his eyes closed. She tiptoed in and took a chair, savoring a sip of coffee while she waited for him. Was he resting or praying she wondered. She wasn't sure.

John opened his eyes and warmly looked at Jennifer.

"I sneaked out to get my coffee fix. I need it because I haven't had a good night's sleep in days."

John politely smiled. It was apparent that his thoughts were preoccupied elsewhere. Without any emotion he asked, "Have you made your decision?"

"Yes. If Scott agrees with you that your evidence isn't enough to indict Dana's dad for murder, then I want him to wire me with the hope of obtaining a confession."

John's heart sank. "Are you sure? Your life would be in jeopardy. I have enough evidence to arrest him for drug smuggling."

He didn't say my life "might" be in jeopardy but "would." "John, it was just a day ago I asked God for His forgiveness and decided to live for Him. That little voice tells me that the right thing to do is to try to help the police convict a brutal murderer. The only reason I wouldn't do this is because of personal fear, and you told me that in your 'world' we shouldn't worry about ourselves."

John's emotions were mixed. He was elated that now she was striving to live for Christ but devastated knowing that her decision would certainly mean her death. John protested, "Personal fear is a little more complicated in a situation like this."

Jennifer interrupted him almost in tears. "John, I made the worst decision of my life not listening to the voice that told me proceeding with my abortion was wrong. That decision has tortured my soul almost to death. Now that same voice tells me that this is the right thing to do even if it means my death. I never want to have that feeling of regret in not doing what I know is right again. I'm sorry because I can see in your eyes that my decision is tearing you apart."

John tried to pretend that he approved of her decision. He forced a fake smile, "I'm proud of you."

Before Jennifer could show her appreciation of his last comment, Scott barged into the room.

"John, I'm glad you're doing better. I must confess I've been kicking myself for not listening to you last week."

Without much emotion John replied, "Don't concern yourself with last week."

Scott continued enthusiastically, "The man who dropped in here last night tried to inject cyanide in your IV bottle. We have his voice recorder, which reveals that he planned on killing you because of some information you have on the governor and Biton's campaign manager."

John didn't share Scott's excitement. "I assumed as much. Will those recordings be made available to the public?"

"Mary asked that we keep a lid on things at the station, but next week that tape will be released. It's part of the Freedom of Information Act. Did this guy kill Dana?"

"No, I don't think he did, but his boss Eleanor would have if she had the chance."

Scott looked surprised. "Did Officer Manuel kill her?"

"No."

Scott leaned forward. "Then who did?"

John explained that Dana's diary revealed that she was blackmailing several people. She needed money to feed her heroin addiction. When she discovered that her dad was in charge of a drug-smuggling operation from Mexico, he became one of her targets to blackmail.

He began to explain how the scheme worked. Once a week, Dana's dad would load a trailer full of old or unwanted horses, even healthy ones whose owners couldn't afford to keep them anymore, and sell them in Mexico. Since horse slaughter in the United States is illegal, it's not unusual to have them shipped to Mexico for slaughter. Once the horses were sold in Mexico, the trailer would be loaded up with drugs in the floorboards.

John showed Scott pictures of the trailer and the special floorboard planking. "See, normally a trailer would use a 2 x 6 plank, but this trailer uses a 4 x 6 plank, which has the core hollowed out. Tubes of heroin are then slid into the floorboards. The boards are then secured when angle iron is welded back in place. Next, the trailer is loaded with cows from Mexico to be transported back to the States. At the crossing, the trailer is ankle deep in manure, which makes the oversized planks undetectable and the fresh welds unnoticeable. The stench from the cows and the animal manure repel the border agents from scrutinizing the trailer too closely and hide the smell from the drug-sniffing border dogs. Every Tuesday evening, a new shipment of drugs would arrive at the sale barn."

Scott was amazed at John's detective work. "That's ingenious."

John reached in his knapsack. "Here's a picture of Officer Manuel at one of the drug drop-offs. Also, these are pages from Dana's diary revealing Officer Manuel's involvement."

"I searched Officer Manuel a couple of hours ago, and I found arsenic on him. I searched his car when I got here, and

I found the spray paint bottle he used to put death threats on the walls of your home."

"Mom will rest easy knowing that the guy who put the death threats there is caught."

Scott continued, "It appears that Manuel wrote death threats all over your home with the expectation that I would place him to guard your room. He hoped this would afford him the opportunity to use the arsenic on you. I should have known something was up when Office Manuel suggested a guard and then offered his help. "

"There was no way of you knowing," John said to placate the situation.

"I know." The thrill of catching the phony nurse roused satisfied emotions in Scott. "Your would-be assassin last night isn't cooperating at all. He's really stupid because the recorder and your IV bottle tainted with cyanide are all we need to put him away for a long time. His boss, Eleanor, will be convicted, too."

John looked at the clock, which read 8:30 a.m. "Uncle Scott, I wanted to tell you all this yesterday, but you were out of town. How long can we keep a secret?"

"We can keep things quiet for several more hours but not days waiting for the next drug shipment."

John smiled. "You don't have to. There's an underground vault in the machine shed beside the sale barn. The drugs are stored there until they're shipped out. Right now, the vault is full of drugs. There's a secret door located under the pallet of sandbags."

Scott beamed with joy. "I can have a warrant in an hour."

Jennifer spoke up. "Detective Peterson, what about Dana's murderer?"

Scott was so excited about coordinating an international

drug bust that he forgot all about Dana's murderer. "John, what evidence do you have that Dana's dad murdered her?"

John explained that the position of the stab wound revealed that she was stabbed by someone who was left handed. The other suspects were all right handed. Since Dana's dad was missing his right arm, he had no choice other than to use his left hand. In addition, whoever stabbed her did so while she was unsuspectedly sitting in her chair. Dana always ignored her dad when he walked into the room, which made him the only person possible to walk up to her without arousing concern."

Scott shifted his glance to Jennifer. "How did Jennifer fit into all this?"

John sighed, "She was at the wrong place at the wrong time."

"Your deduction is plausible but not enough to convict him." Scott turned to Jennifer, "Good news, with all this new evidence, the DA will drop the charges against you."

"Dana deserves that her murderer be pursued." Jennifer noticed that John closed his eyes.

Scott replied, "We win some and lose some. In this case, we might lose the murder conviction but get him on drug smuggling."

Jennifer didn't give up. "Dana's dad goes fishing every Saturday morning and then goes to Jack's Pancake House for an early lunch. This is a weekly ritual that he never breaks. If you wire me, I think I can get him to confess when he returns home at noon."

Scott straightened up, "That would be extra dangerous today. The chief has everyone in the department keeping the governor safe while he is in town. I would have no backup. It would only be me and you doing the sting operation. That would be too dangerous."

The polite smile left Jennifer's face. "I understand, but I believe we need to try it for the sake of justice."

'Justice' was just the right word for Jennifer to use with Scott. He lived for justice in every breath he took. "All right, if you understand the danger, I'm willing to give it a try."

Lord, give me strength! "That will be fine." Jennifer replied insincerely.

"Let's go down to the police station, and I'll brief you on the details of what you need to do."

Mary peeked in the door. "The governor is here to see you, John."

John replied, "Tell him that I'll be ready in a couple of minutes. I'll send Jennifer for him when I'm ready."

Mary smiled at the thought of John telling the governor to wait. "I'll do that."

John returned his attention to his uncle. "Jennifer will be needed here for now. She'll meet you at the police station shortly so that you can discuss the details of the sting. We need to keep everything a secret until noon."

Scott looked puzzled but agreed to John's plan. Without a word, Scott headed out the door envisioning all the bad guys he would put away before the end of the day.

John turned to Jennifer. "You'll want to call your parents and say your goodbyes."

The gravity of the situation started settling in. Jennifer's voice cracked as she replied, "I'll do that."

John looked down at his rosary he was holding. "Good news, Fr. Bob dropped by an hour ago. Mom told him about the murder attempt. He realizes the seriousness of the situation and has agreed to give you an emergency baptism. Do you still want to be baptized?"

"Yes!"

John looked up and forced another smile. "Good, he plans on meeting you at the chapel at 9 a.m. We better get the governor in here so that you can make it."

Jennifer offered John a reassuring look. "John, I know you're worried about me, but I think you can trust your uncle to keep me safe."

"I'm afraid you'll end up just being collateral damage to him."

Jennifer didn't move but stared at John. She grabbed his hand. "John, I trusted you and put my whole life in your hands. I feel like I was an ugly lump of clay that you slowly formed into something beautiful. For the first time in my life I feel happy and at peace about myself. Thank you."

John politely smiled but didn't respond with words.

Her eyes remained fixed on him. "Everyone knows guys don't like sharing their feelings. Sometime in the future, you might regret not sharing your true feelings for me. Know your actions have spoken louder than any words could have ever done. I know my love for you was mutual. I want your happiness, so keep your heart open and one day the Lord will send you the perfect young lady to share your life with."

John was too choked up to speak. He knew Fr. Bob couldn't wait around for Jennifer today, so she had to be in the hospital chapel in twenty-five minutes. The thought of her missing that appointment was unthinkable. "Thank you for those words. We don't have much time—please, get the governor."

Chapter 33

Jennifer introduced the men to each other in a tone that expressed a warm, familiar relationship with everyone present. "Governor Wilson and Mr. Simpson, allow me to introduce you to John Lightman. Peter, I know you already know John. You're going to be very interested in what he has to say."

Once the handshakes and hello's were over, all eyes were on John.

"Gentleman, thank you for coming here." John looked at the governor, "About four months ago, Eleanor Smith met Dana Keller. She offered her money to fund her drug addiction. In return, Dana shared behind-the-scene news regarding you. At first the news was fairly innocent, but Eleanor's fresh supply of new money transformed Dana into a drug addict who would do anything to feed her habit. The deeper Dana sank, the deeper the secrets she was willing to reveal.

About six weeks ago, Dana invited Peter to a movie while Jennifer was out of town. Dana drugged Peter with a date-rape drug and created some very incriminating pictures."

Jennifer interrupted, looking at Peter, "I'm sorry Dana did that to you. I could only imagine the pain it caused you."

"Thank you." Peter felt ashamed of how he'd treated her.

"We've got Dana's laptop and cell phone. To our knowledge, it's the only place she kept the pictures she planned on using to blackmail you. Although we need to surrender Dana's stuff to the police in a couple hours, if you want, I'll let you delete the incriminating picture. The elimination of your files will not jeopardize the police investigation."

Gene jumped into the conversation. "Yes, we'd appreciate the opportunity to delete them!"

Jennifer joined the conversation, "While we're on the subject of laptops and computers, Mr. Simpson, would you please return my phone and computer you stole from my house?"

Gene sheepishly agreed. "Sure."

"Thank you."

"Jennifer, would you like to share the rest of the story with them?" John asked.

Jennifer understood why John thought it would be best if she shared the part about the abortion. "About five weeks ago, Dana found out that I was pregnant. Eleanor offered Dana $5,000 if she could talk me into an abortion and have Peter pay for it. Dana drove me to the abortion clinic and helped me fill out the forms." Jennifer began to cry uncontrollably, barely able to add, "Governor, I'm sorry but I aborted your grandson."

Gene rubbed his chin, "Although I believe your story, what kind of evidence do you have to substantiate it?"

John looked at Jennifer and desperately wanted to hold her, but his injury didn't allow him to move. All he could do was continue the conversation. "Dana had a heroin addiction that needed to be funded. She was blackmailing several people to obtain money. She double-crossed Eleanor by recording her conversations. These conversations are on the computer as well. In addition, Jennifer saw Eleanor give her a large sum of money a couple of days after the abortion, and we have Dana's bank records on her computer confirming a large deposit of cash on that day. Dana also kept a personal diary that contains all this and more."

The governor became encouraged about his election. "Although I wish this could have happened under different circumstances, I'm glad that the evil of the Biton campaign is going to be exposed."

John added, "In addition, the police just arrested an aide to Eleanor who tried to kill me last night. Apparently, he had on him recorded conversations with Eleanor substantiating all this. It sounds as if Eleanor will be arrested later today for being an accomplice to my attempted murder."

"Why would they try to kill you?" Peter asked.

"They found out that I had all of Dana's recordings, which shows their part in their plan to defame the governor. Also, they hoped to obtain the incriminating picture on you, Peter."

Gene pondered the political ramifications. "We need to announce this in our press meeting, in about 2 ½ hours, but it never looks good in the public eye to disclose incriminating information about our opponents. The public would view it as just another political stunt. John, could you lead the press conference? Maybe we could have it in the hospital lobby."

John shook his head. "I'm not really feeling up to it. I'm truly sorry."

"Doesn't matter, I don't think the hospital would let you anyway. You need your rest." The governor looked at Jennifer, "Gene, what if Jennifer led the press conference?"

Gene shook his head no. "She's accused of murder. It would look horrible for her to defend you."

John jumped to Jennifer's defense. "She didn't kill Dana. The police are dropping all charges against her. At noon she's participating in a sting operation to trap the real killer."

Gene reconsidered his objection. "In that case, she would be our next best option."

The governor kindly looked at Jennifer, "Jen, would you do that for us?"

"I'd be glad to." Jennifer said sincerely.

"We can precede under one condition." John said seriously while everyone listened carefully. "There's a police sting at noon. It's imperative that none of this gets out to the public until after the sting is over or else Jennifer might be in additional danger. Agreed?"

"Absolutely." The governor gave Jennifer a fatherly stare.

"Good." John looked at Jennifer, "You have two minutes to make your next meeting. Run."

Jennifer departed for her emergency baptism without saying goodbye. As she ran down the hall, she desperately wanted to know if that 'voice' told John that she would die or if it was just his hunch. Given the certainty of his conviction, she suspected that the former was probably the case.

Chapter 34

Governor Wilson's campaign office was full of reporters waiting for the special briefing. The scandal had made national headlines, so every TV station was represented in addition to all the newspapers from around the state.

The hypocrisy of the pro-family governor being involved in an abortion-murder plot was too good to be true. Although Governor Wilson's connection and some of the facts had been embellished, the media didn't care. Truth was never really the object of the reporters; ratings were. Everyone knew this story was good for the ratings, and they sought to make the best of it.

Many reporters were quietly chatting among themselves waiting for the conference to begin. Others were getting adrenalin rushes as they considered what embarrassing questions they would pose to the governor. All of them knew the story of the year would begin shortly.

With the governor unexpectedly announcing the postponement of his campaign yesterday, most of the reporters in the room believed the governor would announce that he was stepping out of the race. Because there were only four days to the election, a sure victory for his opponent was assumed.

In was 11 a.m. and still there was no sight of Jennifer. Gene hoped she would have arrived an hour earlier so that he could rehearse some answers with her. He gave the governor a worried look. Just then, the office door opened.

"Hi guys!" Jennifer confidently walked into the governor's back office. "Detective Peterson had to prepare me for the sting operation, and it lasted longer than I thought."

"No problem," replied the governor, as he warmly welcomed her arrival. "Should we prep her?"

"No. It's always best not to keep reporters waiting. Also, we have a deadline of forty-five minutes before she's headed for the sting operation." Gene faked a confident look as he turned to Jennifer, "You'll do fine."

He knew there was nothing else that he could do other than hope for the best. Even if she completely screwed up the conference, the story alone should be enough to secure a victory.

The governor gave the order to begin. "Gene, will you announce to the press that Miss Jennifer Lawson will be leading the conference?"

Gene nodded yes. He walked out the door to the podium to fulfill the order.

"Ladies and gentleman, the governor's press conference is going to begin. I would like to remind everyone that each of you present has agreed to remain in this room for an hour after the conference without reporting the contents of this meeting until that time."

"Why the gag order?" heckled a reporter.

"Are the doors secured?" Once an affirmative was given to Gene, he continued, "The police are going to be conducting a sting operation immediately after this conference, and if the contents of this conference were to be reported, it might jeopardize the safety of those involved."

The governor walked quietly to the far edge of the stage with his wife and son. Gene instructed him to position himself as far away from the podium as possible in order to avoid the possibility of being caught in a photo with Jennifer.

"The governor will not be talking or taking any questions.

He has canceled the remaining campaign stops. He plans on being at his home with his family until the election is over."

Another reporter yelled, "So it is true the governor is ending his campaign?" This question and many others went unanswered. Many reporters started voicing their disappointment.

Gene struggled to regain control of the crowd. "At this time I would like to invite Miss Jennifer Lawson to the podium. She will be leading the governor's press conference."

The reporters went crazy asking questions why a suspected murderess would be leading this press conference. These questions went unanswered also as Gene quickly left the stage. He, too, did not want to be caught in a photo with Jennifer.

Ever since the baptism, Jennifer repeatedly reminded herself who she was living for. *Love demands me to do this for God and others.* Filling her head with positive thoughts allowed her to walk confidently up to the podium among the crowd of savage reporters.

Once again in her life, she noticed she was alone. It did not go unnoticed that the podium was on one side of the stage and the governor's family stood on the opposite side. But now that she found herself living in another world, John's world, this abandonment didn't bother her like it would have in the past.

The endless flashes from the cameras were almost blinding. Jennifer stared briefly at the podium, which had fifteen microphones attached to it.

While she waited patiently for silence, she noticed Gene sitting in the front row with a pad of paper. Unknown to her, he wrote the number "-10" on it, which represented the number of points the governor was presently behind in the polls.

The reporters finally conceded to her request for silence.

She looked out to the crowd of reporters and smiled as she began the conference. She purposely stared again at the multiple microphones in front of her and opened with a joke, "Didn't anyone ever teach you guys to share?"

The crowd giggled at her innocent humor.

Gene scratched out -10 and wrote -8.

Jennifer radiated an innocent joy, which captured the hearts of the reporters. "Please allow me to share with you a few more details to the story that's been leading the headlines for the past twenty-four hours. After that, I will take your questions."

Jennifer looked down at her notes. "Last night, at 3 a.m., I was in the hospital room during the attempted murder of John Lightman. The hit man was Jim Hilton, a campaign aide for Charlie Biton. He was sent by Eleanor Smith, Biton's campaign manager, to murder John to help cover up another murder they were part of."

There was a confused look on all the reporter's faces as they struggled to put the pieces together. Someone asked, "Did Eleanor murder Dana Keller?"

"No, I'm referring to their involvement in the death of my unborn child. It was part of a ploy. Eleanor had paid Dana Keller money to obtain embarrassing family information on the governor's family. Dana was a desperate drug addict who needed money. Eleanor paid Dana a $5,000 bonus to convince me to abort my child and have Peter pay for it."

Another reporter interrupted her. "This is unprecedented evil. Do you have any evidence of this?"

Jennifer graciously accepted the reporter's question. "When the police arrested Mr. Hilton last night, they found on him a recorder with conversations between him and Eleanor plotting the murder of John Lightman. The recording revealed they wanted him dead because he knew too much about the relationship between Dana and Eleanor. In addition, they found an empty bottle of cyanide in his duffle bag. I'm sure the forensics lab will soon confirm that cyanide was put in John Lightman's IV bottle, which was witnessed by a person who identified the suspect."

"Why would John Lightman have evidence that Eleanor was secretly plotting against the governor?" asked another reporter.

"While John was helping me prove my innocence regarding the murder of Dana Keller, he discovered motives for several other people wanting to kill her." Jennifer remained posed and confident. "Dana was blackmailing three people to help fund a drug addiction. Although in the beginning, Dana and Eleanor teamed together to plot against the governor, in the end Dana decided to double-cross Eleanor and tried to blackmail her, too. An hour ago, I surrendered Dana's computer, cell phone, and diary to the police, which documents all these accusations. I have just ten minutes for questions."

"How much of a bystander are you in this election? Are you going to vote for the governor given everything you know?"

Governor Wilson stood motionless throughout the press conference. He knew that all he could do was politely stand there and look stately.

A mischievous smile grew on Jennifer's face as she glanced in the governor's direction. "I was warned you guys would ask me trick questions. "I'm sorry, but since I'm only seventeen, I can't answer who I'll be voting for ... Berryville isn't Chicago, you know!"

Laughter filled the room. The reporters felt increasingly attracted to Jennifer.

"Tell us what it was like being an insider in the governor's family. Are all the rumors about the vicious family fights true?"

A thoughtful disposition came across Jennifer. "I must admit that when I would read articles about the governor's family, I would wonder if they were talking about the same family I came to know. Although they aren't perfect, they always hang together, and in the end that seems to be what's most important. I come from a broken family where we didn't hang together. I wish my family was more like theirs."

"Can you tell us what it was like playing tennis with the governor? Also, who usually won?"

Jennifer smiled politely at the trivial question. "Yes, we played a lot of tennis together, but we never kept score. It seemed as though we just chatted about life as much as we played tennis."

"Why would he engage you in conversations about life?"

Jennifer's gentle eyes looked over at the governor. Her gaze returned back to the reporters. "I suspect he enjoyed talking with me because he needed a break from the nonstop political conversations he was used to having 24/7. I sensed deep down he loathed politics as much as I did."

Gene was elated with her reply. Even though he didn't believe a word of it, he considered her reply about loathing politics to be a home run hit with the voters.

Although the reporters hoped for a little 'dirty laundry,' deep down they admired the simplicity of the answers provided by this beautiful, young girl in front of them. She had no guile, which was refreshing after covering political races all year. She came across as a daughter any parent would dream of. "Tell us what kind of things you talked about with the governor."

"It really isn't newsworthy."

"Let us decide," a reporter challenged her as others giggled.

Jennifer used her right hand to push her hair back over her shoulders. "I've made a point to always respect the privacy of the governor's family, and I'm proud to say that I've never divulged anything regarding their private lives." Jennifer gave a wink, "Since I'm sure that I'm just among friends here, I will trust you all with a secret. I'll share with you a sample of one of the topics of conversation the governor and I enjoyed."

"Aren't you late for your sting operation?" yelled the governor.

Jennifer joined the reporters in their laughter of his joke.

She turned to give a warm glance back at Governor Wilson and began her story, "We enjoyed many long conversations over Soozier. Soozier is a beaver that lives down by the river by the tennis courts. I named him Soozier after a punching bag with the same name. No matter how many times you punch this bag, it always returns upright.

It's the same with that beaver. Last summer Soozier endured two floods that destroyed his home. Between the floods, kids 'vandalized' his home as well. Soozier never gave up. He always overcomes everything life sends his way and rebuilds his home.

The governor and I admired Soozier. Deep down both of us wondered if we would always bounce back from what life would send our way like Soozier does. Soozier is my inspiration. I don't know how many times I told myself that if he can bounce back, I can, too."

Gene looked as happy as if he'd won the lottery. Over the past couple of minutes he had scratched out various numbers as he continually took a pulse on the success of the press conference. His latest tally had the governor up by 12 points in the polls. That represented a +22 point swing and a landslide victory for the governor. It was the best press conference he'd ever witnessed in his life.

Changing the subject because of time running out, a reported called out, "So you didn't kill Dana Keller?"

Jennifer's pleasant smile didn't leave her face. "I didn't kill Dana. Detective Peterson dropped all charges in light of the new evidence given to him."

"Then who killed Dana?"

"It's not for me to disclose that information. I'm leaving now to be part of a sting operation with the hope of gaining a confession from Dana's killer."

"It sounds dangerous. Are you scared?"

"I'm scared only when I think about it." After a pause, Jennifer continued in an exasperated tone, "And I'm trying not to think about it!"

The room erupted in chuckles again. Jennifer came across as a genuinely, likeable person.

"You're a pretty girl with your life in front of you. You've dated perhaps the most desirable bachelor in the state. Soon you'll be part of an undercover sting operation to catch a murderer. What's next in your future?"

Jennifer rolled her eyes in jest at the characterization of her life. The reporters melted with her playful gesture. Out of the corner of Jennifer's eyes she noticed Scott gesturing her that it was time to go. "I need to go. My future will be the sacrifice I leave each one of you in this room and the others outside this room. My legacy will be to leave this world a better place for you all to live in."

"It sounds like you think you'll die."

A solemn look settled on Jennifer's face. "When you're all allowed to leave this room in a little more than an hour, I'll be dead."

"Why do the sting, then?"

"We're all going to die one day, but what's most important is how we live. Since I'm the only person who can see that Dana's murderer is brought to justice, I feel it's my duty to try. What kind of world would it be if good people feared doing what's right? Thank you."

Governor Wilson walked over and gave Jennifer a hug while the camera flashed. While they were embraced, Jack said, "You'll be okay."

Jennifer looked kindly into the eyes of the man who had been a father figure to her. "Governor, you're a politician, which means you're an eternal optimist. I'm afraid to tell you, but in this case you're wrong." She ended tenderly with, "Good-bye."

Jennifer was about to exit when she saw Peter shaking behind the platform. She walked over to him and gave him a hug. She whispered in his ear, "I forgive you. You need to forgive yourself and ask Jesus to forgive you as well or your unforgiveness will destroy you. Be strong!"

Detective Scott grabbed her hand. "Dana's dad was spotted leaving Willy's. He'll be home in thirty minutes. We have to go right now!"

Chapter 35

The sound of the Keller's garage door opening reminded Jennifer of her break-in a week earlier. She took a deep breath as she kept reminding herself that she was a precious child of God and God loved her more than she could ever imagine. Flooding her mind with these thoughts dispelled the terror she would have normally felt under the situation. The kitchen door opened. *Dear Lord, help me. I'm doing this as proof of my love for you!*

"What the heck!" was the first thing that came out of Tim Keller's mouth when he noticed Jennifer sitting in his lounge chair with her feet resting comfortably on the footstool.

Jennifer purposely avoided eye contact as she continued to stare at the glass of red wine she was holding in her right hand. "Hello, Mr. Keller, it's nice to see you, too."

Tim immediately pulled out his cell phone, "I hope you're enjoying yourself because in a couple of minutes you're going to be arrested again. Breaking and entering, underage drinking, and I'm sure they will come up with another dozen charges!"

"Just in case you don't remember the number to the police station, it's 589-7200." Jennifer paused and remained staring at her glass of wine. "I can't wait for them to show up so that we can discuss your drug-smuggling operation."

Dana's dad stopped dialing the police. "I don't know what you mean."

Jennifer laughed uncharitably. She recalled that her anger used to lead to irrational decisions. She hoped that if she provoked Mr. Keller to anger, he might slip and incriminate himself.

"That was the worst job of acting I've ever seen. Let me refresh your memory. You slide tubes of heroin in the floorboards of your stock trailer that makes weekly Mexico runs. The drugs are then stored in an underground vault in the machine shed."

Tim Keller walked over and sat on the couch situated near Jennifer. Once seated, he replied, "I'm listening."

A creepy feeling came over Jennifer from being in such close proximity to Mr. Keller. *He suspects I'm trapping him.* She still hadn't made eye contact with him but rather continued to stare into the wine glass. Her gesture of ignoring him was similar to how Dana treated him when he walked into a room, and she knew he hated it.

"Dana and I became close. We shared a lot of secrets, but maybe more importantly, we both serve a demanding Master."

Jennifer paused for Tim to talk, but he didn't.

He needs to get angry so that he'll make a mistake and confess. Jennifer confidently rubbed the top of her wine glass with her index finger. *I wonder if this was the color of His blood.*

Tim's silence worried her as she continued, but she knew what to say to get him mad. "Why didn't you go into Dana's room after she died and destroy her laptop, which contained conversations of you and Officer Manuel? Certainly you also knew that she kept a diary that you wouldn't want others to read."

Jennifer finally made eye contact with Tim for the first time. As soon as his eyes met hers, she continued mercilessly, "Because you're a coward and were scared of the little demons in her room!"

Tim Keller began to fume. "If you have all this figured out, why don't you go to the police?"

Jennifer sensed she succeeded in getting under his skin. She decided to get up and walked over to the living room bay window. There she pretended to stare out the window.

Instead of looking out the window, though, she stared at

the glass she was holding. She poured the glass of red wine as a reminder of the sacrifice Jesus made for her. She considered it her quasi, make-shifted sacramental. Staring at the glass was a source of great comfort for her. *Lord, I'm doing this for you!*

"I need you to get Officer Manuel off my back. Did you know that I might be tried as an adult, so the death penalty could be applied to my case? At best, I'm not too psyched spending the next several years behind bars."

"You didn't answer my question."

Jennifer continued to look out the window. "Detective Peterson has it out for me. Anything I say he uses against me. Screw him and the system. All I'm asking is that Officer Manuel tells the truth about what happened at the scene of the crime—I didn't confess."

Tim took advantage of her back being turned to get out his revolver. "That's it?"

A snap from the gun harness led Jennifer to believe that her end was near. She continued to stare at the glass of red wine. *Lord, will this make up for my abortion?* "Well, two more things. Your little framing job has tainted my prospects to hold a job locally. Certainly a little restitution money would be in order. I won't be greedy like Dana was."

Tim turned off the safety on his revolver. "The second thing?"

"The coroner said the knife was twisted after Dana was stabbed. I know you killed her. What did it feel like for a father, someone God ordained to be the protector of his family, to kill his own daughter? Was it thrilling or did you find killing your own flesh repulsive? Maybe you had a power trip over it. I'm dying to know what you felt when you twisted the knife."

Tim Keller had enough. "It didn't give me nearly the joy this will!"

He confessed, run! Jennifer started running for the door when she heard a gunshot. Simultaneously, she felt a burning sensation in her side. She fell to the ground squirming in circles while blood was flowing out of two holes in her body; the entrance hole and exit hole. She never knew a bullet could burn so painfully.

Six consecutive gun shots were heard by Jennifer, as she formed her last thoughts. She was unsure if she had just been finished off or not. The room seemed to be spinning or was it that she was still squirming in circles. She wasn't sure. Although she didn't feel any fresh pains, she was unsure that if she was shot again she would feel the additional pain. Her present agony seemed unbearable.

Since she sensed unconsciousness was at the door, she decided to pray one last prayer. *Dear Mary, please unite this pain with your Son and win John the grace to find the perfect wife.* The loss of blood made her feel very cold and woozy. The roar of approaching sirens was the last sound she heard.

◆ ◆ ◆

It was 1 p.m. at Governor Wilson's local campaign center, and the reporters were gathered around the police scanner. A microphone was placed at the speaker so that they could monitor the police and ambulance transmissions. In one minute, the doors would be opened and the reporters would rush to submit their stories. Just as the doors were being unlocked, the ambulance paramedic radioed the hospital that they lost all vital signs of Jennifer Lawson. She was dead.

The governor quietly excused himself and wept bitterly in his office. The reporters were in shock as they silently left the building.

Chapter 36

An orderly wheeled John into Jennifer's room, set the brakes, and left.

The two stared at each other.

For days Jennifer wondered how John would treat her now that his sleuthing mission was over. His work of charity was done. Would he still desire her company? Her apprehensions faded as she noticed him staring at her.

John broke the silence with a joke. "You got a lot bigger room than I did."

Jennifer laughed. "I told the hospital administrator that my family couldn't afford it, but he insisted."

"Look at all these flowers! I think I'm in a rainforest." John continued teasing her, "You're the local hero. Actually, your story made national headlines over the weekend. You're famous!"

Jennifer rolled her eyes as she noticed John still staring at her. "Last week, I was called a murderess and this week, I'm a hero. Next week, I'll be forgotten."

"Good, I would hate for all this to go to your head," John kidded.

"Trust me! This is not going to go to my head."

John thoughtfully asked, "So, how are you feeling?"

Looking down at her bullet wound, Jennifer struggled to keep a straight face. "I feel 'holy'."

"That's a sick joke!"

As they both laughed, she added, "I'm sorry, I couldn't resist."

John slowly got up out of his wheelchair and sat on the edge of her bed. Jennifer thought of protesting but knew John only had the most upright intentions so she held her tongue. She seemed very vulnerable because of her bullet wounds; she could barely move.

An uncontrollable cough came upon her so she covered her mouth with a handkerchief. She looked down and noticed a little less blood than her last cough. "Excuse me."

"No problem. I still can't figure out how you got the hospital to agree to me visiting you."

Jennifer looked lovingly into his eyes. "The doctors think I'm not going to make it, and they're being extra nice to me. They granted me what they think is going to be my last wish."

"You think you'll pull through?"

She raised her eyebrows. "Yep! I will enjoy a full recovery. But don't tell anyone, or I'll end up in a room fit for a commoner, like yours."

John laughed. "So you're going to prove the doctors wrong?"

The thought of repeating her convictions seemed inappropriate. She instead just bit her lower lip and smiled.

John took her silence as a yes. "Did you hear Governor Wilson won by twelve points?!"

"I did. He dropped by yesterday and said hi." Jennifer wanted to change the subject to the shooting. "Did Detective Peterson tell you how Dana's dad was fairing?"

"You didn't hear?" John straightened up. "Scott shot him six times shortly after he shot you. Mr. Keller was buried yesterday."

A chill went up Jennifer's spine. She took a deep breath and looked the other way. "I hoped to visit him in jail. He wasn't ready for judgment, and I didn't help him in his last moments."

She's really changed. "Yes, he probably wasn't ready for judgment."

Jennifer just continued staring the other away. She had a blank look about her as if her thoughts were a thousand miles away. John didn't know what to make of it, but thought it was time for him to share his true feelings for her. "Please forgive me for not telling you how deeply I care for you."

A gracious smile came across her face as she returned her look to his eyes. "Thank you. I already told you that your actions spoke those words to me."

"When I thought you died, I felt like a part of me died, too. It was horrible." Tears started swelling as he recounted that moment.

John started slowly leaning toward her to give her a kiss when she pleaded for him to stop. *John, you want to save your first kiss for your future wife!* Once he returned to his previous position, Jennifer continued, "John, I'm not the same person I was before the shooting. I think you need to wait and make sure that you like the 'new me'."

"What do you mean the 'new you'?"

"John, I died. The hospital records show that I lost all vitals for twenty minutes before being resuscitated. I saw the other side, and I'll never be the same person I was before." She noticed he seemed a little incredulous, so she decided to convince him. "When I was at the hospital, my soul departed. Before I left this world I saw you talking to the nurse. She told you I died and left you alone in your room. You started pounding your right hand on the bed rail. You threw your food tray down. When the orderly came to clean it up, he just thought it fell off your bed. I tried to scream to you that I was all right, but you couldn't hear me."

"So you really did die!" John had no doubts since there was no way for her to know those details of his reaction. "What was the other side like?"

Jennifer beamed. "It is so indescribable! The joy and peace are incredible! The beauty is unimaginable! There are so many more colors than we have on earth. It's a thousand times better than your best dream."

"I don't understand. When one dies, he experiences a particular judgment."

"I was judged."

John teased, "No purgatory for you?"

"Nope, I went straight to heaven. I was only judged for the last three hours of my life. My judgment started after my baptism. After going through every detail of the last three hours of my life, I can tell you that it would have been horrible if my whole life was judged. I owe you big time for setting up my baptism!"

John understood that the biggest day of a one's life is the day one dies. Only at this point is an individual's fate sealed for all eternity. Because John lived every day with this in mind, he was fascinated with her story. "Would you mind telling me about the details of your judgment?"

Jennifer pretended to be astonished at such a question. "You're awfully nosey!"

John blushed, "I'm sorry, forget the question."

Jennifer touched his hand. "I'm just teasing. I'd be happy to tell you."

Jennifer caught another cough in her handkerchief. This time she noticed a little more blood than before.

"My judgment started at the press conference. Jesus was very pleased that I only portrayed the good virtues of the governor's family, who were malicious towards me. My actions revealed my complete forgiveness. This pleased Jesus greatly. I was told that my act of charity would influence Peter so much that later in his life it would be the catalyst for him to repent. Without my act of forgiveness, he would never respond to the graces God will give him, and his soul would have been lost. The joy in seeing Jesus satisfied with my behavior was an awesome feeling."

"I saw the press conference on TV. I was so proud of you for how you treated the governor and Peter."

Thank you for telling me you're proud of me. "Then Jesus judged my meeting with Dana's dad. Although my courage to pursue justice in Dana's murder pleased Jesus, how I tried to provoke Mr. Keller to anger to achieve those means was wrong. It is a scary feeling facing Jesus with an unconfessed sin. You have nowhere to hide, and you feel completely exposed."

John looked confused. "Interesting, but how did He handle your sin?"

"He said 'this time' he would look the other way because my only intention was to perform an act of love for Him. He made me understand that through no fault of my own, I didn't know that my act of love was imperfect by not loving Mr. Keller in my actions as well. Provoking him to anger to gain a confession was wrong, but since my motives were not self-serving but rather motivated purely as an act of love for Him, He granted clemency.

Since I am so new to the faith, I wasn't held accountable. It was made clear to me, though, that the next time when I die, I will not be granted this favor." Jennifer paused until John looked her way, "John, will you teach me the faith? I need to know how to love God perfectly. Judgment day is pretty serious stuff!"

"Of course." John's thoughts then drifted to how his life would be seen before God.

After another pause, Jennifer broke the silence, "It's funny, but in the eyes of Jesus, me forgiving Peter was far more meritorious than laying down my life for Dana."

"See, I told you Jesus would forgive you for the abortion!"

Jennifer sighed. "Yes, I was forgiven. I asked Him about the gravity of abortion. He showed me a pit of countless men and women being purged in immense suffering. When I tried to look away from the horrible sight, I saw another vision of numerous damned souls because of the sin of abortion. I was told that a soul with that sin could go straight to heaven if it tried to atone for that sin and tried to develop a perfect love of Christ. But I was also told that very few people have a complete contrition for that sin. It seems with most people there is more remorse than contrition."

"Heavy stuff."

"Let's not talk about that." The thought of being loved unconditionally by God and the souls in heaven overtook her. "I enjoyed a brief walk in heaven. I didn't want to leave because my joy was complete. It was as if I was transformed to the person I was created to be, which was in perfect union with God. I walked around and talked with various people."

"Wow, did you talk to any of the saints?"

"I'm not sure about names, but I don't think so. I was given a privilege to talk with a handful of souls. They were all holy men and woman with one thing in common, humility. They never desired to be celebrated among men for their holiness. When I reflect on my life as the girlfriend of Peter, thrust into the limelight with the envy of all those around me, what a dangerous place for the soul to be in. The cheap thrill of notoriety was a high that I lived on. It's funny that I thought I had it all, when in actuality I had nothing.

I walked around heaven. I met people from all walks of life. There were hermits, souls who dedicated their lives in prayer, tireless preachers, some who spent their life loving the crucified Jesus, some who loved the child Jesus, unsung heroes who were among the countless unknown moms in this world, and the list goes on. One thing they all had in common was not one of them appeared so holy as to bear a halo in the eyes of the world.

I used to pity you because you seemed so quiet and reserved in school. I thought if you would let your wonderful personality shine so that others could see, you could easily be one of the more popular kids in school. How mistaken I was. I have come to see you as the richest person I know because of your friendship with God."

"Thank you for those kind words." John was anxious to change the subject from talking about him. "So, you mentioned I might not like the new you."

"Our exciting days of sleuthing are over. I have no desire to be the life of the party anymore." Jennifer looked out the window. "It seems as though everything in this life is vanity to me now. I want nothing but to do the will of God every moment of my life. Thanks to you, I know the secret to happiness, and I want to be happy."

John leaned toward Jennifer to give her a kiss. Jennifer's injury made it impossible to move. *Help me, Lord, to do your will!* Just as John approached, another uncontrollable cough erupted. Jennifer quickly turned her head to cough into her handkerchief. Jennifer apologized, "Sorry."

John leaned back to his previous position. "Maybe that's God's way of saying that we save our first kiss for our wedding day."

"I think that would please God the most." Jennifer smirked.

Her eyes revealed that there was more to the subject than she was revealing.

"What is it?"

"I'm just thinking about the cruel joke God is playing on you. See, I was supposed to die and not come back, but God answered a prayer in a way I never dreamed." Jennifer started giggling. "When I was lying in a puddle of blood, half dead at Dana's house, I prayed that Mary would unite my sufferings to her Son and send you the perfect wife."

John started putting the pieces of the puzzle together. "You mean ..."

"Yeah, we're a match made in heaven!"

Uncreated Love

If you liked *Saved by a Knife*, you probably will enjoy reading *Uncreated Love* written by the same author

Release Date: March 25, 2016

Amidst life's unrelenting punches, can one be truly capable of a higher love? David and Linda are two high school seniors who are confronted with this challenge.

David, popular and self-assured, is faced with the dilemma of either forsaking a part of his Catholic faith or having a mark against him which has lifetime ramifications. The age old questions confront David: where did I come from and what am I called to be? When he rejects the notion that he is nothing more than a product of the random chance of evolutionary forces, he finds himself in the greatest quandary of his life.

Linda possesses all this world has to offer: looks, friends, popularity, money and a fallen soul. Among her many faults, she has two redeeming characteristics, a rare ability to love completely and her rich sense of humor. When she is forced to consider the option of not living for herself for thirty days but rather to seek God's uncreated love, something unexpected happens.

In a world full of compromises, *Uncreated Love* offers hope that there is promise for man amid such a fallen world in a humor-filled drama.

Go to uncreatedlove.com
Sign up for book discounts and release information!

Top Secret

The sequel to *Saved by a Knife*

Release Date: July 13, 2016

Six years later, John and Jennifer find themselves reunited with the purpose to finally court for marriage. Although they planned to begin courting as soon as John finished college, the war delayed Jennifer's return from a missionary sabbatical by a couple of years. They find themselves back together, but in a faithless and hostile world they do not recognize.

Jack Tipton, a young, single, adventurous, high-level NASA scientist, discovered a secret which has the potential to convert the world. The "powers that be" will go to any length to insure this secret doesn't get out. When Jack is mistakenly assumed to be murdered, he finds himself a nameless man with the weight of the world on his shoulders. The only problem is that he couldn't care less about the world or its conversion. After he realizes that his "top secret" information might be the only thing that can save John and Jennifer, will he make the ultimate sacrifice of his life?

John and Jennifer again find themselves in a page turning thriller that expounds our Catholic faith in their unique and entertaining style.

Go to uncreatedlove.com

Sign up for book discounts and release information!